ERCKMANN-CHATRIAN was the pseudonym used by Émile Erckmann (1822-1899) and Alexandre Chatrian (1826-1890), who wrote most of their works using this collaborative signature. Though they achieved a considerable popular success primarily due to plays and historical novels, such as *Madame Thérèse* (1863) and *L'Ami Fritz* (1864), they are mostly remembered today for their horrific and fantastic tales, which were praised by both M. R. James and H. P. Lovecraft.

BRIAN STABLEFORD'S scholarly work includes *New Atlantis: A Narrative History of Scientific Romance* (Wildside Press, 2016), *The Plurality of Imaginary Worlds: The Evolution of French roman scientifique* (Black Coat Press, 2017) and *Tales of Enchantment and Disenchantment: A History of Faerie* (Black Coat Press, 2019). In support of the latter projects he has translated more than a hundred volumes of *roman scientifique* and more than twenty volumes of *contes de fées* into English.

His recent fiction, in the genre of metaphysical fantasy, includes a trilogy of novels set in West Wales, consisting of *Spirits of the Vasty Deep* (2018), *The Insubstantial Pageant* (2018) and *The Truths of Darkness* (2019), published by Snuggly Books..

ERCKMANN-CHATRIAN

A MALEDICTION

TRANSLATED AND WITH AN INTRODUCTION BY
BRIAN STABLEFORD

THIS IS A SNUGGLY BOOK

ISBN: 978-1-64525-026-5

CONTENTS

INTRODUCTION

THE stories in this volume were originally published in *Histoires et contes fantastiques*, signed "Émile Erckmann-Chatrian" in Strasbourg by the Imprimerie de Ph.-Ale, in 1849. They make up the entire contents of that collection except for a poem entitled "Fantaisie."

"Émile Erckmann-Chatrian" was the pseudonym of two writers working in collaboration, Émile Erckmann (1822-1899) and Alexandre Chatrian (1826-1890). *Histoires et contes fantastiques* was their first volume of prose, although they had published the text of a play the previous year. They subsequently shortened their pseudonym to Erckmann-Chatrian, under which signature they published one volume in 1855 and many more from 1859 onwards, including collections of short stories and novelettes—a few of which were Gothic tales of the supernatural—and numerous historical novels, as well as a number of plays, achieving a considerable popular success until they parted company in the 1880s. It is probable that many of the works bearing their joint signature, especially those written after the Franco-Prussian War of 1870, were written by one or other of the writers rather than both in collaboration; Erckmann is generally thought to have been the senior partner, and the sole author of at least some of the prose works.

Many of Erckmann-Chatrian's works were translated into English in the nineteenth century, with a particular emphasis on their fantastic short stories, which had been reprinted and recombined in France in collections such as *Contes fantastiques* (1868). Of the three stories in the present collection, "Rembrandt" was reprinted as "Le Sacrifice d'Abraham," and translated as "Abraham's Offering," while "Vin rouge et vin blanc" was retitled "Le Bourgmestre en bouteille" and translated as "The Burgomaster in Bottle," but the lead novelette does not seem ever to have been reprinted or translated until 2012, when the appearance of the source text on gallica permitted an electronic version to be issued, confusingly, as *Contes fantastiques*.[1]

The original title of the collection sounds a trifle misleading to modern readers because of shifts in the usage of the word *fantastique*, which did not carry such a strong implication of the supernatural then as it does today. Only one of the three stories is explicitly supernatural, although the mysterious thefts featured in "Rembrandt" are left unexplained and can easily be construed as supernatural at the reader's pleasure. All of the stories are, however, fantastic in the sense that they have a calculated implausibility about them. The tim-

1 The 2012 edition, produced with the aid of optical character recognition, is edited slightly; among other alterations it changes the title of the lead novelette to "Le Malediction," an amendment with which I cannot sympathize.

ing of the book's release might have been significant in determining the choice of a title, as it was issued in the wake of the 1849 Revolution, during the brief period of the Second Republic, when times were exceedingly hard for writers and publishers, especially in Paris; one of the most conspicuous projects of the day was a series of feuilleton serials running in the daily newspaper *Le Constitutionnel* under the signature of Alexandre Dumas, under the collective title of *Les Mille et un fantômes*, and it might be the case that Erckmann and Chatrian, or their Strasbourg publisher, thought it a good idea to imply that the collection was of a similar ilk.

Whatever the reason for the slightly misleading title, it caused a certain amount of subsequent bibliographical confusion. The American bibliographer Everett F. Bleiler, summarizing Erckmann-Chatrian's work in his *Guide to Supernatural Fiction* (1983), having observed the authors' tendency to recycle materials, jumped to the conclusion that the 1849 collection must have been the source text of many of the stories subsequently issued in *Contes fantastique*s and other collections, and that error was copied by many other authors of reference book articles (including me). The original being exceedingly rare, the assertion did not become easily checkable until the text was reproduced on the Bibliothèque Nationale's *gallica* website—by which time, of course, reference books had been driven to extinction by the internet, leaving no scope for correction.

The timing of the publication is also significant in the sense that the lead novelette is very much a response to the issues of the epoch, and might well have run into trouble with the Second Empire's censors had any attempt to publish or reprint it been made after 1851. Erckmann and Chatrian were both fervent Republicans and they formed a political society in Erckmann's home town of Phalsbourg before editing Republican newspapers in Strasbourg, including *La Démocrate du Rhin*, in which "Une Malediction" was serialized in April-May 1849, "Vin rouge et vin blanc" in June and "Rembrandt" in June-July. Many Republican writers—including Alexandre Dumas and Victor Hugo—were exiled after Louis-Napoléon's *coup-état*, and Erckmann-Chatrian suspended their career for some years after a play produced in Strasbourg was banned; when they resumed production prolifically in 1859, they had to be careful not to offend the censors. The possibility of reprinting "Une Malediction" would probably have been swiftly set aside, if they ever considered it, and by the time the Second Empire fell in 1870, the story must have seemed somewhat outdated, not because of its Republicanism, but because of its feverish Romanticism.

French Republicanism during the reign of Louis-Philippe was very closely associated with the Romantic Movement in literature and the arts, and many of its most eloquent spokesmen emerged from that Movement; the interim president appointed to head the Second Republic until elections could be organized was Alphonse Lamartine, one of the pillars of literary Romanticism, and several other prominent writers, including Victor Hugo, were given positions in his caretaker government. There is no surprise in the fact that Erckmann and Chatrian were fervent Romantics as well as fervent Republicans, although they toned down their Romanticism considerably, just as they toned down their Republicanism, as their careers advanced. They retained a Gothic element in some of their short fiction, but played a significant role in "domesticating" the Gothic, helping to lay the foundations of modern supernatural fiction.

In that context, "Une Malediction" is an interesting work. It has considerable links to another strand of neo-Gothic fiction that became popular in the late 1840s, a species of lurid theatrical melodrama that earned the Boulevard du Temple in Paris the nickname of the "Boulevard du Crime" in that era. That tradition never entirely faded away, and enjoyed a second heyday in the *fin-de-siècle* when it became the stock-in-trade of the Grand Guignol theater and borrowed a new generic nickname therefrom. "Une Malediction" is pure Romantic melodrama, and deploys a whole series of narrative moves in its patchwork plot that were later to become clichés of the genre, but were still relatively free of rust in 1849.

The title has a double meaning; although maledictions are uttered in the course of the story, the story itself is a kind of malediction, aimed at the corruptions of society to which Romantic Republicanism aspired, quixotically, to provide ideological remedies. It is remarkably free of restraint in its hectic scattering of narrative devices and its fervent speechifying, and in extrapolating its tragedy to the fringes of nihilism. Erckmann and Chatrian wrote nothing else so flagrantly extreme, and although the French Romantic Movement had no shortage of reckless dealers in quasi-Byronic flamboyance, "Une Malediction" remains unusual in its excess. If it lacks the style of such great posturers as Petrus Borel, Jules-Amédée Barbey-d'Aurevilly and "Philothée O'Neddy" (Théophile Dondey), it certainly matches them for verve.

"Vin rouge et vin blanc," the first of the collaborators' numerous fantastic *contes*, clearly shows the influence of the German Romantic E. T. A. Hoffmann, whose works were very successful in French translation in the 1840s, and retained an iconic significance as French supernatural fiction developed its own tradition in the nineteenth century, taking extensive inspiration from German sources, in syncretic combination with the powerful influence of Edgar Poe. Erckmann-Chatrian's story partakes of the same macabre humor that Hoffmann and Poe routinely deployed in their hallucinatory fiction, deftly alloyed with its horrific element.

"Rembrandt," which was subtitled "Histoire fantastique" when it was serialized in *Le Démocrate du Rhin*, might well have been intended to be a fantasy when it began, but changed tack during its composition. Feuilleton serials were always vulnerable to the effects of feedback from readers, as well as whimsical changes of direction occasioned by the fact that writers were delivering their copy on a near-daily basis and making up their stories as they went along. There was a gap of ten days between the first two episodes of the serial and the remaining four, during which the plan might have changed—and with two authors involved, it is not necessarily the case that all the episodes were written by the same hand. It is difficult to believe that the irresolution and ambiguity of the story's conclusion was planned in advance, and probably the case that it resulted from a fatal uncertainty on the part of the two authors as to how they ought to explain the mystery that they had set up in a casually optimistic fashion.

It was by no means rare for writers central to the French Romantic Movement to employ the lives of painters, musicians and writers as source material for works of fiction, in which they invented freely. S. Henry Berthoud was particularly fond of the stratagem, and had enjoyed some success chronicling the hypothetical adventures of Peter Paul Rubens, and Jules Janin had also joined in with the game enthusiastically and productively in such stories as "Le Diner de Beethoven, conte fantastique" (1834; tr. as "Beethoven's Dinner"). The introduction of a supernatural element into such stories was not unprecedented, as in Janin's "Hoffmann, conte fantastique" (1834; tr. as "Hoffmann") and Delphine de Girardin's "La Canne de Monsieur de Balzac" (1836; tr. as "Balzac's Cane") but it carried a certain risk, and it is understandable that Erckmann and Chatrian hesitated and prevaricated in supplying their story with an ending.

The three stories, seen as a set, are interesting as early work by writers who went on to cultivate a greater fluency and expertise; they feature imaginative seeds that germinated in much of Erckmann-Chatrian's later work, and a certain awkwardness due to inexperience is more than compensated by raw enthusiasm and an unashamed boldness. As contributions to the Romantic Movement, they show an enterprise characteristic of that endeavor, and the precise moment of their composition and publication, during the brief and turbulent historical interlude of the Second Republic, gives them an extra dimension of interest that is shared by few other texts, and could never be repeated.

✳

The translations were made from the copy of the 1849 edition reproduced on the Biliothèque National *gallica* website.

—Brian Stableford

A MALEDICTION

A MALEDICTION

I

What! Go already, the day is yet distant.
Romeo and Juliet[1]

THE moon is rising like a vast opal crescent tinted with a glint of gold . . . the daylight is fading, the noise dying away . . . Liège, the ancient and brave Wallonian city is lying asleep in the mist. Its high bell-towers and its sharp roofs are lost in the shadows. Nothing is any longer perceptible on the mountain . . . nothing except the citadel, perched like an immense aerie at the summit of a rock, darting the eyes of its sentinels over the sleeping city. Even the river is flowing almost without a murmur in its bed of reeds, and attentive nature is collecting herself in order to listen to the vague harmonies of the night.

However, at this advanced hour, a light is still burning down there on the edge of the Meuse, like a star lost

---

1 There is no direct equivalent of this line in the balcony scene, but French translations of Shakespeare were often extremely loose.

on the bank. That flickering light illuminates part of the façade of an elegant white house posed like a bird's nest between large trees and the river. A svelte bold balcony covered in white and pink flowers attaches its gracious girdle to the flanks of that pretty retreat. That balcony is occupied by a young man and a young woman. Leaning on the railings, they are listening silently to the murmur of the waves mingled with the rustle of the foliage.

Suddenly, the clock of Saint Paul's chimes the hour. The young man straightens up. "Oh," he says, taking one of the young woman's hands in his. "Midnight! Midnight already; it's the time of departure . . . of absence. Maria, repeat to me, once again, the melancholy words of amour that you sang yesterday, standing against that great tree with the perfumed flowers."

"You like that melody a lot, then, Karl?" she replied.

"Yes, because it's as sad as my heart when I'm far away from you."

Maria picked up a guitar, and sang in a suave voice:

When the silent shadow of evening comes
I hear her voice
As a sad and pensive sigh passes
In the depths of the wood.

He has gone, my soul is solitary
Light zephyrs
Carry my prayer to his homeland
And my sighs.

18

Old Uldine, Uldine the witch
Said to me one evening:
Why pray, child, if your prayer
Is powerless.

Then, taking my trembling hand in hers,
She sang
The accursed hymn that the frightful sabbat sings
On summer nights.

To see and hear him again for an hour
I would give
Jewels, gems, the crown of Flanders
If I had it.

But I have nothing but my mother's cross,
Her silver cross.
That a brass wire at the end of an old rosary
Still suspends.

If you knew . . . her voice is so lovely,
Her song so soft,
It is the angelic voice one summons
On one's knees.

She fell silent, and Karl, who had listened, pious and meditative, as if suspended from her lips, raised moist eyes to gaze at her.

"Maria," he said, "I love you."

"Karl," the young woman replied, with a touching softness, "five weeks ago I was still a celebrated prima donna. I had bravos and crowns every evening—glory, in sum—but I was sad . . . my soul was etiolated, like a flower lost in the desert. I felt that I was dying. Today, I'm unknown, perhaps forgotten, and I'm happy . . . oh, yes, very happy, Karl . . . I love you too!"

The young man made no reply, but he gazed at her with an eloquence that no human words could translate. For a long time he remained motionless, as if plunged in immense contemplation. In fact, the woman was beautiful! Not the suave German beauty that makes one dream of the first hopes of life; her beauty had a nobler, more serious character. Clad in a somber mantle that designed her slim and supple figure vaguely, a blue dress embroidered with roses outlined her gracious forms more faithfully. Her dark eyes, under the superb arc of her black eyebrows were radiant with a joyful and proud gleam. Her white teeth, like oceanic pearls, contrasted with the velvety brown of her face, and her long ebony hair unfurled over her shoulders and draped her like a second mantle.

Finally, Karl broke the silence. "Maria," he murmured, "you told me this evening that your life is a page of dolors, that you have not found anywhere a heart where your own can repose . . . that you are an orphan. Well, I too have suffered, and I am still suffering, for fatality imposes on me, as a duty, a terrible vengeance. Like you I have sought happiness, like you I have found nothing anywhere but indifference and disappointment. Of my family, only I remain in this egotistical world, Maria. Our destinies resemble one another; we have both wept, we both love. Would you like to be the Comtesse de Romelstein?"[1]

Two tears of happiness shone in the young singer's eyes, but she made no reply.

Karl was there, leaning toward her, scarcely breathing and not daring to raise his head, so much did he fear to read a refusal on his lover's face, so fearful was he, alas, of seeing the last and sweetest illusion vanish like all the rest . . .

A few seconds passed, as slow as centuries, and Maria still remained silent, and Karl waited in an attitude full of anguish and reproach.

Finally, he said, in a dolorous tone: "Oh, my beloved, will you refuse me that word of life? Will you be mine, Maria?"

"Yes," she replied. "For life and for eternity."

Karl detached a magnificent ring from his neck, which he wore in memory, and put it on his lover's finger; then, inclining, he placed his lips, trembling with emotion and happiness, on the young woman's pure forehead.

They withdrew afterwards to the corner of the balcony and sat down in the midst of flowers. They stayed there for a long time, hands interlaced, doubtless talking about the future, speaking in low voices about their dreams and their hopes, and then falling silent in order to listen to the harmonies of the breeze that was weeping in the

---

1 The fact that Karl is German implies that his name and title ought to be Graf von Romelstein, but it was conventional in France to reconfigure such titles in the French style, and I have followed the authors' example.

trees, mingling perfumed flowers with the confused curls of their hair.

The orient was tinted crimson. A few sunbeams passed over the mountain like immense steaks of fire; the stars paled and faded away in the mirror of the river. The young woman stood up.

"Tomorrow, Karl, tomorrow," she said, "I will tell you my entire life."

"Oh! Tomorrow will be long in coming . . . the daylight hasn't appeared yet."

"Yes, Karl, here comes the sun, rising over the fiery mountain. The river is shining between the reeds, the flowers of the night and amour are closing, moist with dew. And up there, the sentinel of the day, the skylark, is launching itself into the sky, singing its hymn to the dawn. Yes, Karl, it's daylight, the hour of departure."

"Already, how long the hours of separation seem to me!"

"Karl," said the young woman, "are you not always near me? Are you not my life, my soul, my happiness? I would be dead if I had not seen you. The moment your love flies away from me will be the last of my life. My soul will fold up like those flowers before the light, and I shall die in order to love you still."

"Die?" said Karl. "Can one die when one is in love, when one is happy? *Au revoir*, my beautiful Comtesse." He brushed his lover's forehead with his lips.

"Adieu, Karl."

"Adieu, Maria."

They quit one another with a happy smile on their lips. The Comte went down to his boat, moored in a corner of the garden, not without turning round many times. As he passed under the balcony in order to reach the middle of the river, a light white object fell at his feet into the bottom of the boat. He picked it up precipitately. It was a white rose . . . a touching emblem of the young woman's amour.

Karl placed that beloved flower over his heart, and then he raised his head and saw Maria, who, leaning over the balcony, was making a gesture of farewell with her hand.

II

> War of drinking, clinking of goblets
> And munitions of the mouth . . .
> By God, my nose will be colored
> Like venison, clink, clink . . .
> *The Bibliophile Jacob.*[1]

A few years ago, the Café des Acacias, situated on the bank of the Meuse, was the habitual rendezvous of the students of the University of Liège.

That estaminet made a fortune in the epoch of which we speak, thanks to the cares of the widowed Madame Depré and her daughter, Mademoiselle Julie.

---

1 Paul Lacroix (1806-1884), who signed much of his journalistic work "le Bibiliophile Jacob," was at the very heart of the French Romantic Movement, a member of all its important cenacles, more renowned as a popular historian and critic than a poet and novelist, although his work was very varied.

Madame Depré, an excellent Flemish caricature with full, plump cheeks and frank and brusque manners, cheered up the customers with her joyful repartee and her loud infectious laughter.

Mademoiselle Julie was a charming brunette with a pale complexion, dark eyes, pink lips and gestures full of an idle sensuality . . . in brief, a delightful person . . . I swear to you . . . for I knew her, friend reader. She was eighteen years old then, and I had the good fortune to be nineteen myself . . . and you have been young too, or perhaps still are, which is infinitely better . . . so you will not laugh if I tell you in confidence that I remarked in Mademoiselle Julie's smile, in her eyes, in her pose and in her brown hair a host of agreeable things that rendered me joyful, which made me laugh, drink, sing, smoke and dance with a truly extraordinary abandon and gaiety of the heart.

In consequence, I had come to knot my cravat in a suitable manner, to imprison my neck in a false collar, to brush my frock-coat every day, sometimes even to prefer the tobacco and strong beer of Madame Depré to the savant elucubrations of our professor.

But let us get back to the Acacias.

One evening in July 1846 there was great rejoicing at the widow Depré's. A large number of students had gathered there to celebrate the departure of Victor Briqueville, one of their comrades, whom the next day's sun would no longer find in Liège.

Let the reader imagine a low, smoky room overlooking the river by way of four large windows that open on to a balcony. That room has for its only furniture a richly-decorated billiard table, a few tables soiled by liquor, chairs and—an essentially picturesque feature—elegant panoplies of seasoned pipes suspended from the walls.

Empty bottles are strewn on the parquet like brave men fallen on the battlefield, in the midst of a profusion of tankards, extinct cigarettes, chipped cups, broken glasses, tattered neckerchiefs and large gray felt hats with black bands, all swimming in a sea of beer, wine, punch and Schiedam. Drinkers *hors de combat* are lying in the chairs and on the tables, in all the poses of drunkenness and slumber.

To the left, near the windows of the balcony, four students are sitting around a round table, where the flame of a superb punch is rising in a spiral; that fascinating light is caressing their red and animated faces with a blue tint.

Mademoiselle Julie, sitting in a corner of the room, is leaning against the lead of a window gazing at the river and murmuring the famous Wallonian air:

You remember my dear comrade
The famous soldier of the great Napoléon

The gaiety seems to decrease with the flame of the punch, when one of the guests suddenly gets up and clinks his cup against his neighbor's.

"Come on, Raoul," he says, indicating the groups of sleepers, "let's drink to the health of the dead."

"To the health of the dead," stammers Raoul, and empties an enormous cup in a single draught; but almost immediately, his heavy head falls back on to the table, and he sighs as he repeats: "To the health of the dead!"

"Rather drink to the health of the living," says the young woman, plunging the sleeper's cup into the bowl.

"You're right, Julie, to the health of our friends Karl and Saabel."

The glasses clink again

"By Saint Léonard-le-Wallon," said Saabel, with a pronounced British accent, "I'd like to know what the comrades are dreaming, who have put their heads under their wings beside their empty glasses."

"Dreamer putting all the survivors to sleep," said the young woman, "rather seek to know what your friend Karl de Romelstein is thinking. Look, wouldn't one think that he's dreaming of the immortality . . ."

"Of the soul?"

"No, of amour!"

A general burst of laughter welcomed that response.

"Of course!" cried Briqueville. "How can one not think of punch and amour in the face of that beneficent flame that rejoices our sight, beside this pretty brunette who warms our hearts? Unfortunately the punch isn't eternal."

"And amour resembles the punch!"

"Friend Saabel, you talk like the late Minerva," said Victor, in a mocking tone.

"It's possible," the other replied, with a hint of conceit. "When I've been drinking, the liquor lends me wit. It appears, however, that it has the opposite effect on Karl. Look, I believe he's asleep now."

"That's strange," said Briqueville, stroking his brown moustache. "And to think that a few weeks ago that

Germanic drinker put ten Templars under the table! What verve! What gaiety! What enthusiasm! It's incomprehensible. For a month his character has been completely different. Offer him a cigar . . . he's dreaming; offer him punch . . . he's asleep. If a joyous song wakes him up, he stares at you with eyes—death of Satan!—with eyes that curdle the joy in your heart. That condition's becoming worrying you know. I can only see one remedy; to get him out of it it's necessary to make a glorious libation of Bordeaux to Dame Melancholy."

"And if the remedy fails?"

"Then, trust me, it's incurable. I classify him in the category of quackers, or lovers."

"Or splenetic Englishmen," said Saabel, laughing. Then he started to sing in a guttural falsetto, beating time with his cup.

> Let the floods of wine flow
> And let my body totter
> Near to falling over,
> Let my lips catch fire,
> And until the bottom of the jug
> My arm will be able to draw.

"Shut up, Saabel," said the young woman. "You'll frighten the nocturnal birds with your voice from beyond the sea." At the same time, she opened the door to the balcony and placed her bare arms on the iron railings.

"Hey, Victor," she went on, after a momentary silence, "wouldn't one think that a man is hoisting himself up on to the singer's balcony?"

"A man?" said Victor, standing up curiously. "Are you quite sure, Julie?"

"Look," she said.

There was no mistake. A man had, in fact, just set foot on the foreigner's balcony. That man, enveloped in a large cloak, turned round to dart a glance behind him, and then opened the door and disappeared into the apartment.

"Hmm! Damn! That's strange," said Saabel, his eyes wide

The sound of an oar cleaving the water reached the witnesses of that nocturnal scene; a boat that they had not noticed at first turned on itself, as light as a cockleshell, and went downriver rapidly.

"Ten bowls, twenty bowls of punch," cried Saabel, "to whoever can tell me the name of that fortunate visitor . . ."

He was about to continue when Victor, putting a finger to his lips, made him a sign to shut up.

"Beautiful Julie," said Briqueville, "our friends are asleep, our heads are heavy, the river is calm; go put a few bottles of Bordeaux in the boat that's moored at the secret gate of the garden."

The young woman went out immediately. At the sound of her footsteps, Karl raised his head, but, not seeing anyone in the room who was showing any sign of life, he let his broad and burning forehead fall back into his hands.

A minute later, the two students had resumed their places.

"Well!?" said Saabel, with an interrogative gesture.

"Well," said Victor, "we know the fortunate lover of the mysterious prima donna."

"We know . . . we know . . . by the soul of the great William, I don't really know what we know . . . that diabolical man in a cloak is as incomprehensible as Maria herself."

"For you, Saabel, yes," replied Victor, while a rapid cloud contracted his features, "but for me . . . no! I've seen that man before. Between the two of us, there's a tombstone."

"A tomb!" said the young Englishman, replacing on the table the cup that he was bearing to his lips.

"I'm saying," Victor continued, in a dull voice, "that that man is as traitor, that that traitor is doubtless the singer's lover, and . . ."

"And you're lying like a wretch!" said Karl, leaping to his feet, pale and haggard, his hands clutching the table.

Victor raised his eyes to look at the comte. By the dull expression of his gaze, he thought that he was drunk, and he went on, addressing Saabel: "So, I was saying that the singer's lover is a . . ."

"I repeat," howled Karl, "that there is no other lover than me, Karl de Romelstein, since Maria is my fiancée, and if your drunken tongue dares to pronounce that pure and virginal name again, I'll break you, you see, as I'm breaking this glass . . . and I'll write cowardice and calumny on your forehead."

Victor stood up.

"In that case," he said, fixing his eyes on Karl, his hand extended toward the other bank, "if you're the fiancé,

29

Comte de Romelstein, the man I saw on that balcony just now must be the favorite . . ."

He had not finished when the young German's riding crop cut his face.

Julie opened the door. "Everything is ready," she said.

"Good," said Victor. Addressing Saabel, he said: "Wake Raoul, friend; he isn't too drunk to see two men killing one another."

Then he went out, inviting Karl to follow him with a gesture.

III

Fatality.

"Have a pleasant excursion. Messieurs," cries the pretty girl.

"Good night, lovely hostess," replies a man's voice, and the boat, having cast off, departs under a powerful impulsion.

Four young men are manning that boat. The first, sitting on the rear bench, has his back turned to his companions. His elbows on his knees and his chin in his hands, he seems plunged in profound contemplation. The nocturnal breeze, which is playing in his blond hair, sometimes covers his pale and handsome face with its locks. The man is young, but he has suffered; the bistre seal of misfortune surrounds his large dark eyes with a blue-tinted aureole, and gives his naturally energetic face an appearance of bitter melancholy.

He is Karl de Romelstein.

Behind him, the inferior part of his body lying in the bottom of the boat and his head on the middle bench, is Raoul Brissart. His mouth open, his gaze dull, his garments in disorder, everything, including his forehead, lost in thick hair, lends his violet-tinted face the appearance of the most profound bewilderment. One might think it the head of the Flemish Kermesse seen by moonlight.

Briqueville is standing at the prow of the vessel, one foot in the boat and the other on the edge, his arms folded and his head bare, he is presiding over the strange excursion. The shadow of his tall stature glides rapidly over the waves; the wind lifts up his brown hair, and the moonbeams breaking over his impassive face illuminate it with a funereal gleam . . .

Suddenly the boat bumped into the corner of a garden.

"What weapons is it necessary to fetch?" said Saabel, leaping on to the bank.

"Pistols," replied Victor. "We're equal in strength."

Five minutes later, Saabel, after having deposited a box in the vessel, resumed his place at the oar, and the boat, instead of following the bank this time, cut straight across the current to reach "the cage of frank amours."

At the same moment a distant voice cast into the silence of the night a few melancholy and dreamy notes. The boat stopped.

"What's that?" said Saabel.

"The prima donna, singing," replied Victor.

The voice recommenced. It was one of those dolorous hymns that a broken soul sings to death when the cup of the future overflows with bitterness. The voice, as pure and fresh as a memory of childhood, drew strange intonations from the inspiration of the nocturnal calm, of an expression impossible to render.

Karl had stood up. He listened emotionally to that well-known voice, which seemed to be awaiting the passage to sing him his hymn of death. His poetic soul dilated, and all the mysterious strings of his heart vibrated in unison with that funereal poetry.

The voice sang, in German:

> *The tomb is profound and silent,*
> *Its edge is horrible,*
> *It extends a somber cloak*
> *Over the homeland of the dead.*

Karl wiped away a tear.

"A song of woe," muttered Saabel.

"To the health of the dead!" said Raoul, extending his arm toward the two adversaries. "To the health of the dead!" His head slid into the bottom of the boat.

They landed on the Isle of Frank Amours. Victor leapt lightly on to the grass; the others followed him, with the exception of Raoul, who was asleep, in a drunken slumber.

After having knotted the boat's rope around a tree trunk, Saabel opened the box that he had brought, took out two magnificent pistols and set about loading them with the utmost care.

Karl, silent and meditative, listened to his lover's voice.

Death has no more echoes
For the song of the nightingale;
The roses that grow on the tomb
Are the roses of grief.

Victor measured the distances.

"Here are the weapons," said Saabel.

Karl turned round, shivering, took a pistol and put himself in the place that the young Englishman had indicated to him with a gesture. He was pale.

Forty paces separated the two adversaries.

Before giving the first signal, Saabel consulted Victor Briqueville with his eyes; the latter's only response was to arm his pistol.

The student clapped his hands.

Karl took a step. "Friend," he said, "I was wrong, put in an anger that you ought to understand. Tell me that you were joking, and all is finished."

"Look," said Victor, and with the barrel of his weapon he indicated the bloody bite of the riding-crop.

"Brother," said Karl, sadly, "do you not know that I am horribly fortunate at the game of death?"

A disdainful smile creased Briqueville's lips. They raised their pistols as they marched toward one another.

At the fifth step the two shots departed.

Karl stopped.

Saabel, trembling like a leaf in a storm wind, looked without comprehending at the scene before his eyes.

Victor had stopped immediately, as if stunned by a violent shock, and then had resumed his march toward his adversary. Having arrived close to Karl, he seized him by the wrist, turned him around, and indicated the singer's balcony with his hand.

"Over there," he said, weakening visibly. "Over there, Baron Jahn de Pirmesense . . ."

He had not finished when the voice of a man was heard, strong, vibrant and metallic, accompanying Maria's sweet song. The two voices sang:

> *The storm has blown over my soul,*
> *My veil is torn;*
> *Where shall I find peace? Where shall I find peace?*
> *In the tomb!*

The voices fell silent and Karl turned abruptly to interrogate Victor. The latter, lying on the grass, his breast pierced by a bullet, was writhing in the convulsions of agony.

Saabel was kneeling down, Briqueville's hands in his, weeping silently.

Karl leaned over, opened—or, rather, tore apart—the wounded man's chemise and put his hand on his heart. It was no longer beating.

"Adieu, Brother," he murmured. "Adieu." Then he raised his head, contracted by despair, and with his arms extended toward the singer's balcony, he cried: "Woe betide that woman! Woe betide Baron Jahn de Pirmesense! Woe betide me . . . Woe . . . because the vengeance of this death will require the blood of all three!"

Five minutes later, Raoul, lying softly on the flowery grass of the islet, was dreaming about punch and mistresses, while the boat, maneuvered by an iron hand, was gliding as rapidly as a tern over the silvery waves of the Meuse.

IV

How shall I kill thee, Iago?

An hour after Karl's flight, a boat was going up the Meuse. By its irregular progress it was easy to divine that it was maneuvering to escape the current and reach the left bank. Scarcely had it operated that change in its direction than another boat, abandoning the post it occupied in an inlet of the river, advanced toward the first.

"Hola!" said a loud voice in the second boat. "Ahoy the rowboat!"

The only response of the rowboat was to veer sideways. The boatman uttered a frightful oath, but softened almost immediately on recognizing the individual manning the other vessel. The two men stood up, and began speaking to one another in low voices.

Their conversation was brief. The boatman extended his hand, examined one by one the three gold coins placed there by the other; then, with a gesture of gratitude, he handed the latter his black felt hat and his gray cloak.

"Is that all?" he said, after that exchange.

"Yes, adieu."

And the two boats separated. One went down the river that it had just come up, and the other went to establish itself under the singer's balcony.

An hour went by. The stars were shining in the river like mysterious diamonds encrusted in the profound waves. The indecisive light of the moon, half-hidden by the clouds, extended indefinitely the silhouettes of the tall trees standing on the bank like sentinels. Flowers opened their rich corollas to the kiss of the zephyrs and the tears of the dew. Cool air descended from the mountains over the dormant plain, and the fisherman, enveloped in his cloak, maintained a complete immobility. One might have thought him a crouching statue.

A man finally appeared on the balcony,

"Are you there?" he said.

"Yes," replied the mariner. "Saint Léonard protect us!"

The unknown man descended into the boat, settled on the rear bench, and let his head fall into his hands; he appeared to be reflecting.

With a vigorous thrust of the oar, the boat took to the open water.

The stranger seemed to be lost in his reverie when a violent commotion made him lift his head. The boat had turned about, and as he was seeking to explain that maneuver, he saw the fisherman, who was standing at the extremity of the vessel looking at him with a strange smile.

"Well?" he said, with a gesture of impatience.

The fisherman took off his hat slowly. The moon, disengaged from the clouds, illuminated the pale face and the bloodshot eyes of the Comte de Romelstein.

The unknown man got up as if moved by a spring. "Oh!" he said. "A specter!" And he covered his eyes with his clenched hands.

The comte started to laugh . . . as Satan must laugh.

"Do you believe in God, Baron?" he said,

"Mercy, Romelstein, mercy!"

"Listen, Jahn," Karl went on, in a frightfully calm voice. "It is two years ago this evening that I swore your death over the cadaver of my brother Ludwig, two years that I have been searching for you . . . two years as long as the centuries of the damned. This evening the demon has thrown you into my path in order to break my last hope. Bless him! On your knees, Jahn de Pirmesense, you are going to die!"

"Pity, Karl, mercy . . . pity . . . I repent . . . yes, I'm a wretch . . . but to kill a defenseless man . . . Oh, mercy . . . mercy!"

And the wretch wrung his hands, wept, sobbed . . . and crawled on his knees.

"Die, assassin!" howled Romelstein, striking him on the head with the oar, which caused him to fall into the water like an inert mass.

Karl leaned over the edge of the boat, breathing heavily, his mouth open and the oar held high.

One minute . . . two minutes . . . three minutes went by. A few bubbles appeared on the surface of the water, and everything became calm again.

The student cast a mute laugh into the gulf.

"To the other!" he said.

A few minutes later, the boat stopped under the singer's windows.

Karl scaled the balcony rapidly and traversed the first room. Having arrived at his fiancée's apartment, he opened the door cautiously

The young woman, her head inclined over her breast, was praying, kneeling before an ivory Christ. The moon illuminated her white dress, her pale face and her black hair with a vague radiance. She was beautiful thus, as beautiful as an exiled angel dreaming of Heaven.

The young man stopped momentarily.

"Demon, oh Demon!" he murmured. Then he continued walking, without her appearing to have heard him. He placed his feverish hand on the young woman's bare shoulder.

"You're praying, Maria?" he said, in a dull voice.

The young woman bounded, proud and angry. "Who are you? What do you want with me?" she said, and her hand reached for the cord of a bell.

"It's me," replied the comte, throwing his hat on to the carpet. "Me. Karl, the brother of the murdered man . . . me, the murderer of Briqueville . . . me, the fiancé of the mistress of Baron Jahn de Pirmesense . . . me . . . me . . ."

And he nailed his fascinating gaze to the young woman, as if to read in her eyes the thought of her heart.

"Oh! Karl, what do these threats mean? Your hand is icy . . . your words are burning like remorse; why are you talking to me about assassination, about murder? Are you suffering, Karl?"

"Are you ready to die?"

"Die Karl? Why to die? Do you no longer love me? Am I no longer your fiancée? In the name of Heaven, Karl, what do you want of me? My God, your gaze is doing me harm."

The comte seized the young woman's arm and dragged her toward the balcony. Having arrived outside he made her fall to her knees.

"Listen," he said. "I was on the other bank when the baron came in here . . . into your room. I was down below when you sang about the tomb . . . over there, where you see that kneeling shadow. That's Saabel, who is weeping over the cadaver of Briqueville, my friend . . . my second brother . . . whom I killed for you. I was there, under the balcony, when Jahn came out . . . Jahn, Ludwig's assassin! The assassin of my amour! Now he's bumping his pale head on the stones of the bank . . . he's waiting for you! You sang your death-song this evening, and you've prayed . . . stand up . . . stand up, woman, you're going to die!"

The flash of a dagger sprang forth under the student's cloak.

The young woman got up. "Karl," she said, "don't judge me without hearing me . . . listen to me . . ."

"Silence, Demon!"

"One word . . . only one word to spare you a crime."

"A crime! A crime! Oh well, a crime . . . it will be the second one today."

"In the name of your mother . . . I'll tell you, Karl . . . !"

"Shut up, woman, you'd lie . . ."

"You believe everything, then?"

"Everything . . . yes, everything, you hear, prostitute . . ."

"Well then, you're right, Karl . . . it's necessary that I die, since I'm culpable in your eyes . . . but one day, you'll weep for my death, for I'm innocent. Only grant me one mercy: that I might see the portrait of my mother once more."

"Go," said Karl. Then he watched her draw away. "It's a holy thing," he murmured, "the portrait of a mother . . .

"Oh, by Satan," he continued, after a momentary silence, "she's even more beautiful this evening than when I saw her for the first time. How her mouth is able to take on a lying smile! How soft her voice is . . . as soft as a seraph's song! And her eyes! Oh, those great dark eyes, as brilliant as the unknown worlds strewn on high. Oh, her eyes hurt me! I believe she spoke . . . no, it's the wind in the trees . . . On my soul, I love her still . . . Never, no never, has the work of Satan borrowed angelic form so well . . . I believe she said that I would weep for her one day . . ."

At that moment a loud cry was heard on the river.

Karl turned round. A man was running like an insensate along the shore of the islet.

"Ah!" said the comte. "It's Saabel crying *courage* to me!" He wiped the blade of his dagger on the palm of his hand and went into the room.

"Are you ready?" he said.

"Yes, Karl. What would I do in this world without your amour? You'll embrace me when I'm dead, Karl; I love you!"

He seized her by the hair and drew her toward him, bent over like a lily whipped by a storm.

"Adieu," she murmured, and, her hands joined over her breast, her eyes closed, she waited for death.

"Angel and demon," said Karl, brushing the icy forehead of the young woman with his burning lips. "Adieu."

He raised his dagger.

But his gaze suddenly fell upon the portrait that the singer was holding in her joined hands. The dagger escaped his convulsive fingers.

He wanted to cry out, but he had no voice.

The young woman opened her eyes. "Oh, Karl," she said, "how slow death is to come. Are you afraid, my love?"

At the pure sound of that voice, the comte suddenly returned to himself. "Who gave you that portrait?" he said, in a hoarse, staccato voice that betrayed the storm in his heart. "On your soul, who gave you that portrait?"

"My mother!"

"You're lying! By Hell, you're lying, you never knew that woman."

"That woman, Karl, is Thérèsa Zanga, the gypsy. She's my mother."

The comte dragged the young woman on to the balcony and showed her with a gesture the sky dotted with stars,

"Listen, woman," he said, "and don't laugh at my grief, for your life is too close to your death. How long is it since you saw your mother?"

"I was scarcely ten years old when, one evening, in a street in Aix-la-Chapelle, a man abducted me and took me to Italy."

"Oh, accursed, accursed!" said the comte, his fists raised toward the sky. Then he added: "And you haven't seen her since?"

"No, for it's twelve years that I've been weeping for her, her and my beloved brother Karl."

The student shuddered and leaned on the iron of the balcony.

"Listen, Maria," he said, in a voice as sad as a coffin song, "your mother died weeping for you. I dug her grave myself, because she was said to be damned. I prayed over the damp earth of her grave for a long time . . . and then I quit the Burscheid, taking that ring, which the poor woman had given me an hour before her death . . . the only thing that she could leave me . . . me, Karl . . . me, the son of the gypsy!"

The comte opened his arms to his sister.

They remained thus for a few minutes, both mute, not even daring to raise their eyes, so formidable did the future seem to them.

They finally separated, and the comte, after kneeling down, took one of the young woman's hands in his, which he moistened with tears.

"Sister," he murmured, "can you forgive me?"

The young woman raised her eyes to the sky. "Karl," she said, in a grave and melancholy voice, "get up . . . look at your sister . . . and give her a farewell kiss . . . for she is dead to this world!"

V

And glory! Vain noise that in the noise expires,
Atom in which the sun is mirrored for an instant
And which the sea breeze then carries away,
Crown in which the laurel hides a frightful thorn,
Angel who plunges a dagger in your breast,
A name on a stone and desire to one side!

One evening in January 18** a compact crowd gathered in the vicinity of the theater of Aix-la-Chapelle.

Numerous groups formed around the posters, and it was easy to recognize, by the noise of the discussions and the multiplicity of the gestures, that all those good Germans were taking a serious interest in the advertised performance.

At that moment a young man, whose eccentric costume denoted a British origin, traversed the square. He went like a veritable idler, bumping into some and splashing others—unintentionally, of course—while enduring with an imperturbable calm the more-or-less emphatic *Ahs! Monsieurs!* and *Imbeciles!* that his passage provoked.

The crowds formed near the theater undoubtedly intrigued him, for he drew closer to them; aiding himself with his elbows he was soon facing a poster on which he read:

> *Today, 5ᵗʰ of January, the first performance of* The Mask of Satan, *by an anonymous author.*
> *The principal role will be played by a foreign artiste.*

The Englishman bought a ticket with the nonchalance particular to gentlemen, and went in. The performance commenced in the midst of a profound silence.

Have you ever reflected, reader, when, while walking along the street, poor and silent, a rich carriage splashes you as it passes by, on the matter of social antitheses?

Have you ever noticed the scornful smile of a marvelous person in yellow gloves at the sight of your dented hat or your frayed trousers?

Have you ever wondered what the word "justice" signifies with respect to the millionaire thief and the disdain of the poor but honest worker?

Have you ever been hungry . . . hungry enough to curse life, to break your skull on the corner of a wall?

Have you ever said to yourself then that a lord throws away on his whim of a day what your sweat cannot earn you in ten years?

Have you ever sat at the hearth of a poor man, while the father, worn out by fatigue, undermined by need, is dying on a meager bed while the mother weeps and the children ask for bread?

Have you encountered in the evening on street corners, the pale young women who sell their bodies by night . . . also for bread? I don't say their soul, because they no longer have one. Have you understood that those sad creatures, with a good education and the legitimate price of labor, could have been, if not happy, at least pure and reflective?

Well, if you have seen, thought, reflected and suffered—if, in sum, you are a human being, you will understand what *The Mask of Satan* was.

It was certainly not one of those works made like a Harlequin's coat out of a thousand poorly combined pieces. Nor was it a drama cast in the mold of our pretended grand masters, one of those indigestible compositions in which the intention is all the merit. Nor was it a vaudeville, or a comedy, or a melodrama, or even a tragedy . . . but it was all of that—which is to say that instead of depicting a corner of society and illuminating it in accordance with the demands of fashion, the author had grabbed civilization entire by the collar. He had torn away its frippery, undressed it, from the beggar who holds out his hand at the street cornet to the rich man who spends millions to entertain his stomach, his horses and his mistresses.

It was a work passed through the crucible of a soul on fire, which seemed to have been written with a dagger dipped in lava and bile.

The people found that sublime; respectable people found it charming. No matter—they clapped their hands too, pretending not to see that they were there on the stage, garrotted, side by side with their vices, and face to face with their turpitudes. They clapped their hands . . . I even think that they wept! It was touching!

Thus, when the last word came, when the actors bowed to salute the public, thousands of voices cried: "Author! Author!"

The curtain went up; a great silence fell.

The stage manager advanced, leading by the hand the actor who had played the leading role. That man was pale and his sadness seemed great in the face of that enthusiasm.

"Monsieur Karl Zanga, the author of *The Mask of Satan*," said the stage manager, in a loud and clear voice.

"No," responded a young man leaning over the edge of his box. "No . . . but Karl de Romelstein!"

The author raised his head and recognized Saabel. His knees buckled, and the stage manager received him in his arms as he fainted.

Hands clapped . . . voices cried out . . . crowns rained down . . .

Poor Karl!

VI

Is he rich?
Yes . . .
Oh, the worthy man!
Conversations between civilized men.

The next day, Saabel received a voluminous letter sealed in black; he opened it precipitately. This is what he read:

THE LIFE OF A MAN

I do not know the place of my birth, but when, bruised by the present and disgusted by the future, I descend into the past as far as the first of my dreams, I see myself running through the narrow and somber streets of the old city of Serenus Granus and Charlemagne.[1]

---

1 Local legend had it that the waters of Aix-la-Chapelle, which Charlemagne subsequently made his capital, were first discovered by a Roman named Granus, said by some to be the brother of Nero, while others claimed that the Roman in question was Serenus Granus, an envoy of the emperor Hadrian.

Aix-le-Chapelle, therefore, is my homeland, since it is the homeland of my first memory, my first hope, my first joy and my first grief.

My mother was a poor gypsy singer. Her name was Thérèsa. She was a tall woman, pale and silent. She was still young in the epoch of which I am speaking, for she was scarcely thirty years old, and yet she would have been thought to be at least fifty. Hair as white as the moss of old oak trees escaped from her brown hood, partly veiling her forehead, furrowed by deep wrinkles. Her meager and bronzed cheeks, her severe profile, her thin lips, always contracted by a dolorous pressure, her eyes fixed like an eagle's, but black and hollow, gave her physiognomy one of those strange characters that come from reflecting dolor and pride: a fantastic mirror that the soul understands and speech cannot define.

There was nothing left of youth in that old woman of thirty, nothing but her tall and proud stature, her rapid gesture, her shining eyes and her voice, as pure as a dream of childhood, but sometimes imprinted with a pitiless irony.

She often walked for hours, her arms folded and her head inclined over her breast, in our paltry mansard, from which the view extended over the Burscheid.

And we played, my sister and I, and ran happily—yes, happily—around the little room, narrow and dark. We did not know, we poor children, that our mother was sad; we did not understand all the bitterness there was behind that wrinkled brow. We were unaware of the past; the present, for us, was joy; and the future . . . oh, the future! . . . that was tomorrow's games.

Sometimes, it happened that in our noisy running we bumped into the silent promenade of our mother. She stopped then, raised her head, and saw us at her feet. She leaned over slowly, kissed us on the forehead with a soft smile, and then straightened up in order to resume her interrupted march and her sadness.

Later, when, bitten in the heart by disillusion, I wanted to search my soul for the vague perfume of the early years, that tall woman appeared to me as the genius of hatred presiding over the sweet joys of my childhood.

Thérèsa sometimes took us with her in her nocturnal courses. We went from café to café, my sister and I, singing the old ballads that our mother had taught us.

Those days when we went out were the most productive. Everyone gave to Maria, everyone brought her their obol of admiration and pleasure; everyone wanted to know that gypsy girl, still a child and already as savage and beautiful as the poetry of those old ballads.

The winter of 18** was somber and glacial. My mother, whose energy alone had sustained her thus far, fell dangerously ill. From then on I understood her life. Poverty was the host of our days, dolor came to give a phantom to all our nights. Lying on a camp bed, scarcely clad in rags, the poor gypsy woman was even sadder and more silent than usual. Indifferent in appearance to all our cares, she seemed lost in an abyss of dolorous reflections.

Although I was a child I understood that prompt help was required. One evening, Thérèsa was asleep. We had exhausted all our resources; I took a guitar that was hanging on the wall and I turned to Maria. She had divined my intention, for she was ready. We went out silently, fearing to wake our mother, who had forbidden us to go out alone . . . and yet, help was necessary.

As we went past the Frederick the Great brasserie, I heard a confused sound of voices and clinking glasses from within.

"Let's go in," I said to my sister.

The room was full; I played a prelude of a few deep notes and silence fell. Then Maria started to sing a very sweet and touching ballad that the gypsy woman had taught us on the first day of her illness—a ballad called "A Mother's Heart."

My sister's voice, tremulous in the first couplet, took on from the second a force and flexibility that I had never known her to have. She sang, the poor child, as the angels must sing, imploring the pity of God. Nothing else could be heard in the room but the monotonous sound of the clocks. Necks craning, motionless and silent, all the drinkers, half-drunk, seemed to be under the influence of a magical admiration. One might have thought that a silvery bell was chiming the hour between two gusts of a storm. When Maria had finished, all the hands clapped, and a man that I had not noticed in the crowd advanced toward her. The man was wearing a strange costume; he was tall and handsome. A long black beard fell over his breast. He took Maria's hand gently.

"Who are you, my beautiful child?" he said.

"Thérèsa's daughter, Monsieur."

"Ah! And it's your mother who teaches you music?"

"I've never learned, Monsieur; the gypsy doesn't know it either."

The stranger looked at her for a few seconds with an expression of surprise and admiration. Then he said: "And what is your name, if you please?"

"Maria, Monsieur."

The stranger brushed my sister's hand with his lips, and then straightened up, calm and grave.

"Child," he said, in a slow and solemn voice, "you will be a queen one day, not by virtue of a scepter, but by virtue of the omnipotence of genius!"

Scarcely had he pronounced those words than he enveloped himself in a cloak and went out. No one knew the man.

A few minutes later we resumed the route to the Burscheid, glad to be able to take our mother something to calm her suffering, for we were rich. Before leaving, the stranger had put a large gold coin into my hand.

I knew that, in spite of the result of our excursion, the gypsy would reproach us, so I started to run as fast as I could in order to arrive first and to support our mother's reprimands on my own.

I went up the steep and tortuous stairway precipitately; having arrived at the top steps I paused for a few seconds in order to get my breath back. I pushed the door gently. My mother was sitting up on her bed, pale, her lips blue and her head tilted. I ran to kneel at her feet.

"Why did you go out, Karl?" she said to me, in a dry tone.

"Because I saw that you were suffering, Mother, and that there was no bread."

She let her head fall on to her breast. "Where is Maria?" she said.

"She'll come up, Mother, but" I added, "don't scold her . . . it's me who made her go out."

Thérèsa took my hand and put it on her forehead. It was burning!

"You're suffering, Mother," I said.

"No, Karl, I'm no longer suffering. You have a noble heart, my child. But go to bed, for it's already late."

I lay down on my straw mattress, resolved to stay awake, but fatigue soon vanquished my feeble childish determination, and a few minutes later I was profoundly asleep.

Suddenly, a cold and sinewy hand seized my right wrist. I got up with a bound and uttered a cry of terror. Facing me was a woman. In one hand she was holding a torch and with the other she was gripping my wrist, and I felt as if I were caught in an icy vice. Her black dress was white with snow, her breast and neck were bare; a convulsive tremor agitated all her limbs and her eyes were burning with a somber fire through her long white hair, which was dangling over her face. It was my mother!

"Where is your sister?" she said to me, in such a heart-rending voice that I understood everything. I collapsed on my bed without responding.

"Where is your sister?" she repeated, leaning over me as if to rip the thought from my head. "Wretch! It's you who have lost her!" And two tears furrowed her cheeks, hollowed out by suffering. I was the first time I had seen my mother weep. It seemed to me that those two tears were blood.

I got up and I told her everything: our departure, our ovation at the Frederick the Great brasserie, the stranger's gold coin, and our return. As I spoke I felt her clenched fingers relax. I shut up and I knelt at her feet to beg her for forgiveness. I took a flap of her dress in my hands and as I raised my head I felt two warm tears fall upon my face. Alas, it was the baptism of woe!

"Where is the gold?" Thérèsa asked me.

I took the coin the stranger had given me out of my pocket. She took it and threw it into the street. Then she raised her long and fleshless arms slowly. There was not a star in the sky, and the wind of the storm blew snow in her face.

"Oh, cursed be that man! Cursed be the man who has stolen my child!"

The torch went out, and I heard a body hitting the wall, or falling on the floor.

VII

Have you had a mother?
Do you know what it is to have one?
Victor Hugo.

The day was beginning to break when my mother came out of her faint. She scanned the room with her extinct gaze, and, seeing me beside her camp-bed, made me a sign to approach.

"Karl," she said in a voice broken by suffering, "I'm going to die. In an hour you'll be alone in the world, and you're still very young. Listen to me, then, my child, and keep in your heart the last words of Thérèsa, your mother. You've seen me sad . . . old and broken at thirty years of age . . . and perhaps you've wondered whence comes the gypsy's chagrin, why her hair is white like this . . . The reason, my son, is that in your mother's soul there is a great hatred and a great dolor . . . it's because I am Thérèsa and your father's name is the Comte de Romelstein!

"Your father is a coward. Search for him; he ought to be in Berlin. Go to find him and tell him that, sitting on her death-bed, Thérèsa cursed him. Then, when you have grown up, depart for Italy; it's there that you will find your sister. Remember that the man who has stolen her is your mother's assassin. But it's necessary that before avenging me you learn to suffer; it's necessary that your eyes have no more tears! Tears, you see, make men pity! Tears are for the weak and for cowards!

"You'll grow up alone, thinking about your mother. You won't tell anyone that you're suffering, that you're unhappy; you will be proud under rags, as I have been proud under shame and ignominy. One day, you will stand up strong, for your isolation will have matured you, and you'll have become a man.

"Pose yourself one goal, march there without worrying about obstacles. Fear nothing . . . nothing but weakness and cowardice. If, one day, you buckle under adversity, if you feel your courage weakening, remember Thérèsa, and you will get up strong, like her.

"Adieu. Tell Maria that I died weeping for her. The cold of death is chilling me. Take this ring when I am dead; it was my mother's; wear it next to your heart. Adieu, poor child . . . think about the gypsy who has suffered a great deal, and who is bequeathing you a hatred and a vengeance!"

She fell silent. I raised my eyes; her head was tilted over her breast, her mouth open, her eyes dull.

I knelt down and I wept.

Two days after my mother's death I left Aix-la-Chapelle, no longer happy, no longer indifferent, no longer the Karl of games with Maria, but sad and dejected, my heart drowned in bile.

A few moments of great dolor had made a man of the child. Thérèsa's two tears had initiated me to woe, and her adieux had taught me hatred.

I walked for two days, sad and shivering, the image of that tall pale woman looming up in my heart, and her last words under my brow. I reflected on the abyss that Thérèsa's death had just hollowed out between my past and my future. Then the image of Maria passed pensively before my eyes. I saw her beautiful face framed by her long black hair; shreds of melody and the strange notes of her old ballads sometimes came back to me . . . alas, all those songs were as sad as the memory of my sister, and those notes as profound as my despair . . . Then I stopped to wipe away my tears; for I was weeping . . . yes, I was weeping, in spite of Thérèsa's words; but I was alone. I did not have to fear either disdain or pity.

All those bitter memories were soon joined by others. I recall the response of the priest I asked to bury my mother: a priest proud of his soutane, in flourishing health, happy to feel himself living well.

"Your mother," he said to me, "has no right to a Christian sepulcher. It would be a sacrilege to implore divine mercy for the soul of a pagan. In any case, what would be the point? Hell does not return those it devours. The gypsy is irrevocably damned, and the Church has no prayers for the damned."[1]

That response of the man of God evoked that of the man of the world.

The owner of the house in the Rue Burscheid, after having sequestered Thérèsa's rags and harp, threw me out, saying that he was not stupid enough to confide a room to me, the rent for which he knew it would be impossible for me to pay. I was ten years old then, and the winter was rigorous.

I also recall the indifference of all those men who saw me, a poor child, crouched with despair over my mother's coffin. I saw them turn their heads, doubtless in order not to be disagreeably affected.

Each of those thoughts tortured my heart.

What a frightful lesson those two days contained for me! How the illusions of my childhood fell, young and withered, under the words of that fanatical priest, that egotistical bourgeois and the indifference on the faces of all those civilized men!

Involuntarily, I murmured the gypsy's words: "You who are suffering, sing and you will be welcomed; weep and you will be rejected."

It was in the midst of those painful reflections that I advanced toward Cologne. I had lost sight of the towers of Jülich a long time ago. The cold was intense. I often

_____

1 Authors' note: "This type is fortunately rare among the French clergy."

stopped in order to turn my back to the north wind that was cutting my face. Thin garments scarcely covered my numb limbs, and sometimes I sensed an odor of snow and ice rising to my brain.

Night fell; a few rare stars showed themselves in the somber blue of the sky; the moon appeared, sometimes hidden by thick clouds with snowy flanks, bizarre in form, sometimes uncovered, pale, pouring its wan rays over the silent landscape. The plain was deserted. Nothing could be heard but the plaint of the wind in the trees and the barking of farm dogs, which seemed to be responding to the moaning of the wind.

That bleak mourning of nature, the bitterness of the wind, and all those funereal thoughts stirred up by grief and hunger, depressed me so much that I was tempted to sit down on the edge of the road and await death.

I stopped, indecisively . . . but suddenly, Thérèsa's words presented themselves to my mind; I was ashamed of my weakness and I continued on my way, fortified by the supreme energy that despair gives.

Having arrived at a bend formed by the road at the base of a slight elevation, I perceived a large black mass lying in the plain; it was Cologne. I sat down on a milestone and raised my hand to the sky. No situation, time and place was ever more appropriate to inspire profound meditations; my soul seemed to break its chain and grasp its liberty again momentarily. To the right, the Rhine was flowing in the plain. One might have thought it an immense boa constrictor making its green-tinted scales shine in the moonlight. To the left, arid snow-covered fields went to fade away in the depths of the horizon; at intervals, the eye discovered in that monotonous extent a few paltry plants, and a few stunted trees curbed by the north wind. At my feet was the old city of Cologne, gripped by one of the arms of the river as if by a circle of bronze, presented an impenetrable mass to my sight, from which bright sparks sometimes escaped. Those fugitive gleams caused to spring from the shadows, here the ridge of a roof, elsewhere the corner of a tortuous and dark street; further away were the thousand fantasies of a Gothic portal, its ogives, its moldings, its fleurons and its niches, where the neglected idols of the Middle Ages nestled.

That spectacle made me forget my suffering. I wanted to get up again, but all my efforts to do so were futile. The cold had paralyzed my limbs completely. I was no longer suffering; only my will remained, but it was impotent to shift an inert body. I was there, on that milestone, a short distance from the city, five minutes from life, like a man under the knee of his murderer when the dagger is raised and he sees belated defenders running in the distance . . .

I darted one last glance full of hatred at the old city, and I closed my eyes.

At the same instant, a carriage harnessed to two magnificent horses passed by like a hurricane . . .

It was my last hope. I made a supreme effort and stood up, uttering a long cry of dolor . . . but my strength was exhausted and I fell unconscious on the ice of the road.

VIII

> An eternal sympathy flowed from one to the other.
> *Auguste Luchet.*[1]

When I came round, I found myself in a sumptuous room, lying in a bed so soft and so rich that I thought for a few minutes that I was the victim of a dream. The poor are subject to those sad illusions; they sometimes procure the enjoyments of luxury and softness . . . but they fear the awakening.

The uncertain light of a winter day filtered through thick cashmere curtains.

A magnificent chandelier illuminated the apartment.

Beside me, two men dressed in black were standing. One was small, old and bald, cold and reflective in appearance; the other was young and slim, with an aristocratic physiognomy, but full of kindness and generosity. Long blond hair fell in uneven curls around his face, and his big blue eyes expressed the frankness of a noble character. That man was eighteen years old at the most, for a light down scarcely shaded his cheeks and his upper lip.

The old man took my hand, placed his thumb gravely on my wrist, and remained motionless in an attitude of reflection.

"Well, Franz?" asked the young man, after a moment of silence.

---

1 The ardent Republican Auguste Luchet (1806-1872), exiled for five years after the July Revolution of 1830, author of the quasi-autobiographical novel *Frère et soeur* (1838), was jailed for two years after publication of his novel *Le Nom de famille* (1842) for "incitement to hatred and contempt of the government."

"He's saved, Monsieur le Comte," replied the old man, raising his head with a satisfied expression. "This potion will restore the circulation."

And he put a rich Bohemian goblet to my lips.

"Poor child," murmured the young comte, taking my hand. "My friend," he said, in a soft voice, "What is your name?"

"Karl, Monsieur."

"Only Karl?"

"Karl Zanga."

The young man shuddered and looked at the doctor, who had gone very pale. Then he said: "Where were you coming from, my friend, when you were found by the roadside?"

"From Aix-la-Chapelle."

"And you were going all alone like this in such rigorous cold!"

"It was necessary . . . I'm alone in the world . . ."

The young man enveloped me with a gaze full of such great affection that I was moved by it.

"What about your mother?" he said.

"She died three days ago."

"And your father?"

"I'm looking for him."

"What is your father's name, my friend?"

"Comte de Romelstein."

The old man, after having looked at me for a few seconds with the greatest attention, turned to a portrait of a man suspended from the wall.

"It's him," he said, inclining his head. "It's really him . . . the poor orphan."

"And what do you want with your father, my friend?" asked the comte, in a voice trembling with emotion.

"Nothing," I replied.

"Nothing? But you're young and you're poor; why are you looking for him, then?"

"To tell him that, sitting on her death-bed, Thérèsa cursed him."

A frisson ran over the comte's hand.

"Poor woman," said the doctor, inhaling a strong pinch of snuff. "Poor woman! Proud and unfortunate to the end."

"Karl," said the young man, in a tone so affectionate that I looked at him with astonishment, "Karl, you have suffered a great deal."

"Oh yes," I replied, involuntarily, "we've suffered a great deal."

The comte wiped away two tears; then he said: "You've been very unfortunate, Karl, and yet you're young . . . you haven't deserved to suffer. Cold, hunger and poverty have raged against you; dolor and hatred have embittered you profoundly; your mother, at the hour of her death, bequeathed a malediction to you . . . a malediction against a father! That's very heavy to bear!

"Do you understand how terrible that word *malediction* is? Thérèsa was proud, she refused the comte's help; she refused it for herself and for her children. She died of poverty, died rather than recoil before a duty! She was a noble woman . . . a woman great among them all. You've seen her suffer, Karl, and you've embraced her hatred against your father. But do you know that the man she has cursed shed tears of blood over Thérèsa's pride? Do you know that he knelt before her, in order to ask her to see his son and his daughter, to hug them to his heart just once, before dying, and that she rejected him?

"He wept then, that man . . . he wept a great deal, for he understood that the woman was right. He had played with her; she returned disdain for perfidy. That was justice.

"Poor comte, he suffered a great deal when, in the hour of his agony, he asked for his children and did not see them, when he understood that it would be necessary to die without seeing them . . . and he knew that they were poor and unfortunate! Oh, yes, it was a long and terrible expiation! He invoked Thérèsa, he begged for the last kiss of his children, and Théresa did not come. He died in despair! And now that he is sleeping under his tombstone, will you curse your father's ashes? Will you break the truce of God and cast your anathema upon his cadaver?

"No, you won't curse the old comte, for that would be to curse me too, his son—me, your brother, Karl!"

That man was young, he was good, he talked to me with sobs in his voice—him, a rich man; him, the Comte de Romelstein, to me, a poor gypsy—he mourned Thérèsa, he called me his brother! I fell into his arms, open to receive me.

We embraced for a long time, while the old doctor wiped away his tears and searched for words.

Finally, the comte stood up, and parted the curtains with one hand, enabling me to see the portrait of a man who resembled us.

"Karl," he said, "this is the image of our father."

"Yes, Brother," I replied, "and this is Thérèsa's ring."

IX

Valiant young man, here you lie, lifeless,
seized by the night of the tomb on the
threshold of the nuptial chamber . . .
Retain an endless groan next to the one
who is in eternal silence!
Schiller.

I linked myself intimately in Heidelberg with a young man who, like me, was following courses at the university.

Similar tastes had brought us together, a similar worship of great and liberal ideas had cemented that union, which increased every day in gentle effusions.

Victor Briqueville had suffered a great deal, and although young, he had touched many social wounds with his finger. The son of a democrat spared by the popular ax in 1792, he had inherited from his father a fiery head, a heart entirely devoted to Republican ideas, a name forgotten by the Empire but to which the Restoration had given a new luster by putting it in the pillory of aristocratic opinion.

Proud of the slightly savage glory of his father, Victor had quit France in order to seek friends and dreamers in Germany.

One day I received a letter from Ludwig; it announced his impending marriage to me. *Brother*, he said to me, *we have lost a sister, another sister is rendered to us. Come and be happy with us.*

Poor brother, I had a great place in his affections.

The next day, Victor and I quit the old university of Heidelberg. Our voyage was rapid, for we entered Cologne the following day at noon. Ludwig had gone out in the morning with Franz. No one could tell me at what hour he would return. I ordered the domestics not to tell the comte that I had returned; I wanted to surprise him.

Scarcely was I installed in the house than I heard a loud noise of wheels under my window, and Ludwig's carriage entered precipitately. I launched myself to meet him; I opened the carriage door happily, with a smile on my lips.

For a moment, I remained clutching the metalwork of the carriage, my mouth open, without discovering a cry.

Two men were before me, one lying on a banquette, his body collapsed, his arms dangling, his eyes dull and his breast inundated by black blood, the other motionless, his face distraught, his eyes haggard. I put my hand to my forehead; ideas were shattering in my head; a cold frisson ran slowly through my limbs. I dared not believe . . . it was frightful . . . as frightful as a satanic dream, and yet, it was true!

I took Ludwig's body in my arms and carried it through the consternated domestics. I deposited it on the same bed over which, a few years before, the noble comte had held out his hand to the poor gypsy. I leaned over him to find one last spark of life in his breast . . . nothing . . . he was dead.

As I got up, I saw Franz standing on the other side of the cadaver.

"Who has killed my brother?" I cried.

He looked at me coldly without responding.

"Who has killed my brother? Who has killed my brother, do you understand, old man? I'm asking you who has killed my brother!" And I placed Franz's hand on Ludwig's bloody breast.

At the contact of that cold flesh, the doctor suddenly returned to himself.

"Oh, Ludwig," he murmured, in a stifled voice. "Poor Ludwig . . . dead! Dead! Woe betide Baron Jahn de Pirmesense! Woe!" Then he fell into an armchair, hiding his face, inundated by tears, in his hands

At that moment I heard a panting respiration behind me; I turned round and I saw Briqueville holding his hand out to me silently. I threw myself into his arms and hid my tears in that embrace.

"Friend," he said, indicating the cadaver, "Ludwig's shade demands a bloody funeral."

We shook hands mutely, both filled with the same thought, and we went out, darting one last glance at the comte.

The same day I obtained half my vengeance. Baron Jahn de Pirmesense had fled, but his witness Mathoël lay on the bank of the Rhine, writhing in the convulsions of agony.

Before restoring his accursed soul to Hell, the wretch confessed that he had only charged my brother's weapon with powder, and that the infamous treason in question had been agreed between the baron and himself in order to elude the hazards of the combat.

I had the last honors rendered to Comte Ludwig de Romelstein, and, standing on his tomb, I swore to avenge him.

That same evening I embraced Victor and I left. For a year I traveled Europe, seeking Baron Jahn everywhere. No one had seen him; even those who knew him intimately did not know the place of his retreat.

Finally, weary of that pilgrimage of death, wounded in the utmost depths of the soul, embittered by the hatred and fatigue of my isolation, I decided to return to Germany, and to await there the vengeance that seemed to be fleeing me.

I stopped for a few days in Liège; that city suited my sadness: its old churches, its narrow streets, the high mountains that surrounded it, the cordial frankness of its inhabitants, everything spoke to me with a friendly voice, everything seemed to know me and to sympathize with me.

One day I was climbing the Montagne Saint-Gilles with difficulty when a man seized me abruptly by the hand. I raised my head and I fell into Victor's arms. That year had not aged him. We sat down on the grass halfway up the hill. I was happy and sad to encounter the only friend I had in the world.

"Friend," he said, "you're suffering; dare you not confide half of your troubles to me?"

I shook his hand.

"Yes," he continued, "you're suffering, I can see that by your pale face, your profound gaze, and your bitter speech. You're suffering alone, you love your suffering, egotistically, perhaps you'd like to die of it? You'd like to rest your fatigued head on a tombstone. You'd like to sleep, and you haven't lived! Oh, Karl, are you so afraid of life, then?"

"Friend, I only dread the immense void of my soul."

"Ingrate," he said, with an affectionate smile. "What, then, has made you doubt amity?" He fell silent momentarily, and then he added: "Listen; the great hour is about to sound; the dawn of peoples is shining on the horizon, darting its first light over the ruins of the old world that is crumbling. The swords are drawn; would you like to be one of ours?"

"Brother," I replied, "take my arm to defend your cause, but leave my heart; I need it in order to hate."

Together, we went down the narrow path that winds around the steep flanks of the mountain.

After that, I tried to stun myself; I resumed ardently the noisy life of a student, readapted myself to that atmosphere of beer and cigars; I set down the burden of my hatred for a few days, and tried to relegate my most painful and my dearest memories to forgetfulness. In sum, I mingled with the petulant youth following courses at the University of Liège.

The proof smiled on me; recommended by Briqueville I was received everywhere as trustworthy; all hands opened to shake mine, the most intimate secrets were unveiled to me. For a month I believed in the possibility of a new existence. But I did not take long to perceive all the ridicule and emptiness there was in that permanent state of conspiracy, in those ineffectual speeches in favor of the suffering and the starving, those interminable political discussions stirred up between a pipe of tobacco and a tankard of beer, in that superabundance of words and that sterility of action.

I understood, dolorously, that among all those young enthusiasts, very few had the consciousness of the ideas of which they were the spokesmen; I finally divined that play of marionettes, the principal threads of which ended in the hands of the police. I needed to shrug my shoulders; I thought I had entered into a vast conspiracy and I woke up in the midst of the fumes of a smoking-room.

That was a bitter disappointment; that drop of bile revived all the wounds of my soul, the past appeared to me even more formidable; now it was thrown like an abyss between all illusion and me.

My resolution was prompt and decisive. I wrote a letter to Briqueville begging him, as a last service, to have a grave dug for me alongside Thérèsa's.

I searched my heart for the memory of all those I had loved, I recalled my suffering. I reread Ludwig's letters one by one, the last above all, in which he talked to me enthusiastically about his future. Then I put a few grains of a violent poison into a cup and I opened my windows in order to see the sky.

The evening was superb; the sun was declining majestically behind the Ardennes, its last rays illuminating the façades of edifices; a few vaporous clouds were fleeing to the horizon, and nature was somnolent in the sound of a thousand crepuscular harmonies.

There was such a perfume of sadness and melancholy in that scene that I felt drawn to enjoy it for a few more minutes. I went down to my boat and opened the sail to the gentle breeze. I sat down at the prow in order to dream.

Slight tints of crimson colored the crests of the mountains, but the shadows of the night were extending over the plain. The moon, that mysterious companion of the silence, broke its crystal radiance on the surface of the river; the sounds died away one by one like the last sighs of an organ falling silent. Sometimes the wind carried over the water a few shreds of a distant song, the buzz of an insect in the long grass of the bank, or the fearful twittering of a little bird. The finger of God settled over nature and slumber deployed its fantastic wings in space.

I took off my hat in order to pray.

Suddenly, the words of a song of dolor, combined with the plaintive vibrations of a harp, passed like a breath over the crests of the waves. That voice, of an ideal purity, rising in the midst of the silence, seemed to be taking possession of its empire; the evening breeze held its breath, the boat was still, the waves ceased to murmur. No sweeter impression had ever descended into the depths of my soul. In that poetry there were revelations so profound, harmonies so strange, a resignation so true that I sensed two tears rolling from my eyelids, sterile until then.

The song ceased, and I raised my head. On the bank of the river, in the midst of tall trees, a woman clad in white was standing; her hands, still extended over the quivering strings of the harp, had ceased to draw chords therefrom. She seemed to be lost in an immense reverie. To tell you that the woman was beautiful, that her long black hair, delivered to the breeze, fell back over shoulders as white as alabaster; to tell you that she resembled one of the sublime creations of Murillo, the Spanish painter with the somber and proud touch, or, better still, an angel of dolors weeping over the bitter disappointments of life, would not give you an idea of the limitless amorous enthusiasm that suddenly took possession of my being.

The boat touched the bank; I stood up in order to bend my knee before that divine apparition.

"Oh," I said to her, "Angel or woman, who has initiated you, then, to the words of great suffering?"

Here I shall stop . . . of all that scene, all that remains to me is the confused memory of an indescribable joy, a happiness such as my dreams had never offered to my delirious imagination. The gaze of that woman was reflected in my gaze, her breath slid over my forehead like the warm breath of the night over a plant etiolated by the burning sun. Sometimes, too, I felt the light curls of her black hair fluttering over my face.

Maria loved me!

Oh, what poet, the sublime surges of what imagination could define those three words: she loved me? What human tongue could translate that fever, those aspirations toward the beautiful, toward the infinite? What soul of fire could cast in a mold of bronze or plaster the incandescent metal that is called amour? Maria loved me!

There was a month of happiness, a month of amour, a month filled like a century of existence. Regrets, dolors, despair, my entire life and my double vengeance, everything . . . everything was forgotten. The death of Thérèsa and the murder of Ludwig, were no longer anything for me but a painful dream, the memory of which I rejected, as importunate to my happiness. I wanted to live now, I no longer had the strength of hatred. As egotistical and cowardly as a parvenu, I no longer knew anything but happiness.

But Heaven is just . . .

One evening, I woke up to the sound of an orgy. There was a cadaver at my feet. That cadaver was that of my best friend. Alongside that cadaver there was a woman kneeling and praying under the flash of a dagger. That woman was my sister.

X

Delirium.

Forward! Forward! Halt! Forward! Hell, it's a frenetic course; remorse is pursuing us, but it can't catch us, its steely claws close on empty air. Forward, forward, forward!

Oh, the superb charger of despair! How it bounds, how it launches itself proudly through space, its nostrils casting their foam over the brambles of the path. It raises a dust of stars from the granite flanks, but it cannot shake off the sublime hope that is attached to its black mane . . .

Out there, a squall of demons passes in the mist; white phantoms follow them hectically. Is that justice or vengeance? No, it's fatality. Courage, accursed ones, courage! Our fate is the same . . . Brothers in crime, brothers in torture, courage!

Trees, rocks, brushwood, everything flees, everything disperses before the murderer. Black rocks open their profound caverns to engulf him. That torrent is howling, foaming, and swirling at the bottom of the precipice and singing a hymn of death. Forward! Forward!

The hills whiten, the horizon fades away; it's the mirage of the desert. Oh, that memory, it's indefatigable, it always pursues me, always. And yet I've crossed mountains, ravines, abysms. The torrent has become a river, it flows slowly in the plain, it murmurs, imprisoned in a bed of moss and reeds. Here is an immense avenue, further away a secular cross, and then an old tower corroded by saxifrage. The charger is only advancing awkwardly, its fetlocks weakening. Poor animal, more rapid than lightning, you cannot save your master again; but rest, we're on the threshold of the convent, it's here that Maria has fled.

My sister was waiting for me. She descended a few steps and came toward me; I sat down on the pedestal of an antique statue, my forehead in my hands.

Maria was standing, sad but resigned; she spoke to me for a long time about her life, a page steeped in tears and yet beautiful and gilded in the eyes of the world. She told me her dolors, her humiliations and her deceived hopes one by one, and when she had unrolled that shroud for me, in which nothing remained but ash, I found myself very miserable before that martyr. Yes, very miserable, and above all paltry. I understood that there are sources of bile in women that a man cannot know, fibers that he cannot divine, a pride that he cannot understand.

There was an instant of silence . . .

"And Jahn?" I said to her, raising my eyes.

"Ah, Jahn . . . yes . . . the last link in my chain. He was the director of the theater in Naples when I made my debut there. Enthused by my talent, he made me magnificent offers. I refused his gold and left. For some time I thought that I was free of his pursuits, but he soon reappeared. I gave the order not to receive him in my house. He introduced himself into my bedroom by night like a thief. He begged me with joined hands, in the name of my glory, to resume the floral crown. I was inflexible. Then he asked me, as a supreme favor, to sing him a German poem that he loved. And then . . ."

"And then," I added, coldly, "I killed Baron Jahn de Pirmesense, the murderer of my brother, Ludwig de Romelstein."

Without responding, Maria shook the cord of the cloister bell forcefully.

The door grated on its hinges like a diabolical snigger, and closed again immediately.

I found myself alone in the world.

XI

A funny body, not so?
A madman?
Yes, a veritable madman!

The Léonsberg is a historic mountain little known to tourists; its savage crest dominates the plain from afar, thrown like a titanic step at the base of the gigantic stairway of the Vosges.

A popular legend alleges that the celebrated pope Leo X was born on that rock,[1] and tradition surrounds the birth of that pontiff with a thousand bizarre tales. At any rate, the Léonsberg is a very curious mountain for the antiquarian and the dreamer.

A somber mass of ruins, armored by ivy, rises above the brushwood and the long grass. The enclosing walls are no longer more than twelve or fifteen feet high, but in the center stands the square black tower of the keep. At every step one bumps into fragments of statues scattered in the heather like the bones of an immense skeleton. A bronze Christ stands on the edge of the rock.

Behind that heap of granite is a little white and simple chapel. Imagine, in the midst of those ruins covered with moss and scarred by lightning, a construction having the form of a studio, the door of a cabin and the ogival windows of a château. The architect, who was doubtless a village curé, has pillaged the carcass of the feudal manor remorselessly. Of something imposing he has made something ridiculous.

On seeing from a distance that little white hovel grimacing Gothically, one might think it an honest bourgeois dressed up as a knight.

An old hermit exploits the chapel and the ruins. He is a man about sixty years old, with a jaundiced face, a white beard and hair: a typical Alsatian, with a flat head,

1 This seems unlikely, as Leo X was the second son of Lorenzo de' Medici, nicknamed the Magnificent, of Florence. The mountain in question, the name of which is nowadays spelled without the S, is now best known in the name of a breed of dog, the Leonberg Vosges.

a square face, a broad chin, prominent cheekbones and a hooked nose. Eyes of a singular vivacity shine like two ardent embers in the depths of their orbits. In brief, Brother Niclausse is an old man with a malicious air, ugly rather than handsome, like many old men, for men do not resemble stones; time does not sanctify them, it degrades them.

At the top of that mountain, therefore, there is an old manor, old statues and an old Christ, all bronzed by the centuries . . . that is the work!

Then, alongside, on the same granite base, there is a man, a little chapel, scraped, washed and daubed . . . that is the parody.

Brother Niclausse has an entirely aristocratic ignorance; he cannot read, which does not prevent him from posing gravely before the open missal, sometimes upside-down, and singing at the top of his voice things that he does not understand.

In spite of that lack of instruction, the hermit of Léonsberg is, in the eyes of everyone, a "holy man." He kneels at the foot of the of Christ to say his rosary; before eating he makes eight or ten signs of the cross, and he also begs bravely, like the true hermit that he is. Add that he confesses every week, that he gets on well with the curé of the commune, and very well with the bigoted old women on the mountain, with whom he loves to chat one-to-one over a pitcher of old Wolxheim wine.

That is Brother Niclausse! He is a man like any other . . . but I'm mistaken; the worthy guardian of the Léonsberg enjoys one other quality that is entirely Dutch; he is excessively fond of cleanliness, and threatens to bleach the old Christ . . .

Brother Niclausse is, therefore, also a man of progress.

I arrived in Léonsberg one evening in the month of June. The location pleased me. There were mountains and silence there, old stones and memories. The world only appeared in the distance, in the depths of valleys. For the superstitious pagan, that mountain was the desert; for me it was life. I begged the hermit, who was my cicerone, to cede me a place in his abode for the night. A grimace was my response; the good monk was not hospitable. I tried the supreme argument between civilized people.

"For my place at your hearth," I said to the brother, slipping a gold coin into his hand. He bowed deeply and responded with a further grimace, which this time strongly resembled a smile

I had discovered the holy man's idol.

I put down my traveler's staff in the ruins and I settled on the mountain. I occupied a small oblong room in the keep, constructed of enormous carved stones. Daylight only arrived in that redoubt through a loophole impeded by an enormous bar. Numerous inscriptions covered the stones; they were words of rage or saintly resignation, engraved with tears and chains on a granite page. A ring, brown with rust, attested to the philanthropic procedures that the Comtes de Léonsberg employed with regard to their prisoners.

Brother Niclausse, whom my liberalities had prejudiced in my favor, brought me the day's subsistence every morning and then disappeared, only to reappear in the keep at rare intervals.

I surrounded myself with an impenetrable solitude. I inscribed my name on the stones of the cell, in the midst of all the others. It too was a name of dolors! Then I took a pen and I tried to produce the thought that was torturing my heart. I traced the plan of a drama. I searched my entire life in order to extract all the necessary bile and scorn therefrom. I animated the hero of that terrible work with all my hatred. I dipped my pen in the lava of my memories and I recounted with a poignant irony what I had learned about society. I laid bare all the wounds of egotism; I showed the shame on the insolent velvet of riches, the cowardice on the face of pride. I pursued my goal with a savage indefatigable perseverance; I founded myself in the crucible of that work; I expended therein more than courage, more than talent, more than genius . . . I expended my soul.

Three months spent in that furnace aged me by twenty years.

In the evening, when all was silent, I climbed the stairway that took me to the top of the tower. I sat down on the head of the keep alongside a clump of eglantines. A few birches clung to the fissures of the walls, swinging their funereal arms over the Léonsberg. The wind wept like a thousand dolorous voices as it was engulfed in the loopholes. I dreamed then, my head in my hands, while my soul descended bitterly along the path of my vanished days, like a voyager lost in the desert, searching the sand for footprints effaced by the simoom.

When dawn came, and the songs of the birds, I shook the dew from my damp hair and descended to resume my labor.

My solitude was rarely troubled. Sometimes, however, curious tourists rapped on the door of my coffin with the pommel of a cane.

"What is this?" they said.

"A door, Messieurs and still solid," replied the voice of the hermit.

"What is behind it"

"A dungeon . . ."

"A dungeon?"

"Yes, a kind of sepulcher, in which the comtes locked their prisoners."

"Open the door, then."

"Pardon, Messieurs, but . . ."

"Hurry up; it's interesting to see, a dungeon."

"It's just that . . ."

"Well, what?"

"It's impossible."

"Impossible? Why? You don't have the key?"

"No, Messieurs."

"Ah! Who has it, then?"

"The man who lives in the room."

"What did you say?"

"The man who lives in the room."

"There's someone in there?"

"Yes, Monsieur."

"A man, in this sepulcher?"

"Yes, Monsieur."

"And you know him?"

"I bring him the day's nourishment every morning."

"And what is the man's name?"

"I don't know."

"You don't know him, then?"

"He has never told me his name. I've never asked him for it."

"Why not? You aren't curious . . . ?"

"Yes, but it's because that man isn't like any other."

"Ah!"

The voices were lowered then, and I heard nothing more but whispers mingled with exclamations of surprise. The brother was doubtless telling the visitors a terrible story, of which I was the hero.

Why should the man not exploit dolor? He was exploiting God.

One day, especially, the *ahs* were so numerous, accompanied by such frank bursts of laughter that the idea occurred to me of knowing those tourists laughing with such a perfect grace alongside a man buried under ruins. I went down to the hermit's cell, therefore; it is there that a ledger is deposited in which tourists inscribe their names. I opened it in haste and I read in large letters: *Comte Raoul de Brissart and Comtesse Julie de Brissart, his wife.*

I was about to go out when I heard a loud voice outside saying: "You're right, my love, the madman of these ruins also wants to play the mysterious, like Maria. What the devil can have become of her?"

"And Karl too?" said a female voice.

"Oh, that imbecile Karl; he'll doubtless have ended up breaking his head. Individuals of his stripe always end up that way . . . and it's no great loss . . . misanthropes are even worse than madmen. That hothead! He nearly got me into a nasty affair with his duel. Phew! How diabolically hot it is here!"

I went back up to the keep. The student Brissart and the Liègeoise waitress, transformed into aristocrats, went down the stairway carved into the rock. Two horses were whinnying at the bottom of the mountain.

The travelers seemed very happy.

Alas, poor Raoul!

I wrote the last line of my drama on the twentieth of September 184*

I signed the work and broke my pen.

XII
Epilogue

> The rogue!
> The monster!
> What luck that he's captured
> Indeed . . .
> (*Sentimental conversation.*)

It was, I believe, in the early days of the month of May. The sun was casting its golden dust over the façades of the somber edifices. In the old market square in Liège a scaffold stood, with its beams black with blood and its steel blade scintillating in the distance like a star.

The tortuous streets were disgorging an immense ragged crowd into the square; the balconies were garnished with the most brilliant society, the young women there were all dressed up; proud dandies were scanning the heads that extended into the distance with their opera glasses.

That fine society and that rabble had come to see a man guillotined.

They waited for nearly an hour, quivering with impatience and licking their lips. Finally, a cart surrounded by troops slid slowly into the middle of the crowd, like a skiff over the muddy water of a marsh. Then there were cries of enthusiasm, bravos, and a frenetic joy. They had feared, the worthy folk, that the execution might have been put off.

The Romelstein bastard was standing on the cart. His neck was bare, his breast uncovered, his hands tied behind his back; to his right was a kneeling priest, to his left the black-clad executioner. The priest was pale, the executioner's face was very red. The bastard was calm and cold, like a man who knows all of life and who is only waiting for death. A bitter smile glided over his lips, however, when he heard the crowd howling; that cry of jackals made him shudder; he had hoped for indifference, he found rage.

"I was right," he said to the priest. "It's to do honor to a man to call him a tiger!"

"Forgive them," said the priest. "They know not what they do."

"What use is my forgiveness," said the bastard, with a scornful smile. "I can't avenge myself."

"It's for you, my brother, for your salvation, that the forgiveness is necessary," replied the ecclesiastic.

"You're preaching egotism to me," exclaimed Romelstein, and his eyes sparkled with indignation. "In fact," he said, with a poignant irony, "you're giving me friendly advice; the forgiveness doesn't engage me to anything; it's skillful politics."

The priest lowered his head.

The cart was still advancing. A profound silence fell as the procession passed. A few words reached the condemned man; he collected them as the last adieu of a world in the face of eternity.

"What a rascally face," said an old physician. "The bump of crime is developed in the head in a frightful manner."

"And the bump of theft also," added a usurer, "but he lacked the opportunity."

"He's afraid," said a coward.

"He looks at you brazenly," said a prostitute.

"It's doubt that doomed that man," said a philosopher.

"It's envy, base jealousy, that has killed that wretch," said a critic.

Karl uttered a burst of Rabelaisian laughter as he set foot on the scaffold.

"The wretch is mad." said the priest. "He didn't want to confess, nor take communion; he laughs in the presence of death, his soul is damned for eternity!"

And the priest made the sign of the cross three times while the executioner's assistants bound the bastard to the board.

Can you hear that shiver passing through the crowd like a gust of wind over the crests of waves? It's the horror of death weighing upon twenty thousand breasts, suspending twenty thousand breaths. Not a cry, not a sigh, not a murmur . . . the silence is frightful . . . And then, can you hear . . . out there . . . out there . . . far behind the crowd, that organ weeping like the voice of a dying man? My God! It was, I believe, the last thoughts of Weber, sublime, heart-rending thoughts, like the adieux of a man of genius to a world that did not understand him.[1]

Karl heard that music. Oh, what sad memories, what bitter disappointments flooded his brain then! It was his mother's song! He saw the poor gypsy again, he also saw his sister, and their little mansard, where hunger, cold and poverty came to torture them. He regretted all that; yes, he regretted it, and also the world, with its mockery, its disdain and its injustice.

His entire life was summarized in a few plaintive notes; he felt a tear running down his cheek, he could hear his heart bounding in his breast, his blood seething in his veins; he felt the hands of the executioners gripping his limbs . . . then the beams vibrating . . . a sharp pain . . . a flash . . . annihilation!

Perhaps eternity.

Shall I tell you about the crowd, whose members went home sad and pensive?

About Madame la Comtesse de ***, who returned to her town house drawn by four superb horses;

---

1 Carl Maria von Weber (1786-1826) was the most significant pioneer of Romantic music, much admired by Richard Wagner. The reference is presumably to his final opera, *Oberon* (1826).

Monsieur le Marquis de ***, who smoothed his moustache, saying: "After all, he was a proud rogue; he died without flinching";

Or Monsieur Janotis,[1] who cried: "Human justice is satisfied . . . the murderer of Baron Jahn de Pirmesense will no longer soil the surface of the world!"

No. Our drama is concluded.

---

1 *Janot* was a slang term for a simpleton, most often encountered in the derivative *janotisme*, a stupid remark.

RED WINE AND WHITE WINE

I have always professed a high esteem, and even a sort of veneration, for the noble wine of the Rhine; it sparkles like Champagne, it warms like Bourgogne; it soothes the throat like Bordeaux; it fires the imagination like Spanish liqueurs; it renders us as tender as Lacrima Cristi; in sum, above all, it enables dreaming, unfurling before our eyes the vast field of fantasy.

Toward the end of autumn in 1846 I decided to make a pilgrimage to Johannisberg. Mounted on a poor nag with hollow flanks I had disposed two tin-plate pitchers in its vast intercostal cavities and I traveled in short daily stages.

What an admirable spectacle was that of the vineyards! They were the most beautiful days of my life. One of my pitchers was always empty, the other always full; when I quit one hillside there was always another in view. My sole regret was being unable to partake of that pleasure with a veritable appreciation.

One evening, as night was falling, the sun had just disappeared at the horizon but it was still launching a few stray rays between the large vine-leaves. I heard the trot of a horse behind me. I veered slightly to the left in order to let it pass, and to my great surprise I recognized my friend Hippel, who uttered a joyful exclamation as soon as he perceived me.

You know Hippel, his fleshy nose, his mouth adapted for wine-tasting and his triple-stage belly. He resembled the good Silenus, the follower of the god Bacchus. We embraced enthusiastically.

Hippel was traveling with the same objective as me; he traced our itinerary through the vineyards of the Rhingau. Sometimes we called a halt in order to give the accolade to our pitchers and to listen to the silence that reigned in the distance.

The night was considerably advanced when we arrived before a little inn nestling on the slope of the hill. We dismounted. Hippel darted a glance through a little window almost at ground level. A light was shining on a table, and beside the lamp an old woman was asleep.

"Hey!" cried my comrade. "Open up, Mother."

The old woman shuddered, got to her feet and came to the window, where she stuck her wrinkled face against one of the panes. One might have thought it one of those old Flemish portraits in which ocher and bistre dispute priority.

When the old Sibyl had distinguished us, she grimaced a smile and opened the door.

"Come in, Messieurs, come in," she said in a quavering voice. "I'll go and wake my son; be welcome."

"A peck of oats for our horses, and a good supper for us!" cried Hippel.

"Good, good," said the old woman, hastily. She went out and we heard her climbing a staircase more rapidly than Jacob's ladder.

We stayed for a few minutes in a low and smoky room. Hippel ran to the kitchen and came to tell me that he had observed the presence of several quarters of bacon.

"We'll have supper," he said, caressing his belly. "Yes, we'll have supper."

Floorboards creaked overhead, and almost immediately, a robust fellow dressed in simple trousers, bare-chested and his hair unkempt, opened the door, took four steps and went out without saying a word to us.

The old woman lit the fire, and butter started to sizzle on the stove.

The supper was served. A ham was placed on the table flanked by two bottles, one of red wine and the other of white wine.

"Which would you prefer?" asked the hostess.

"It's necessary to see," replied Hippel, presenting his glass to the old woman, who poured him the red wine. She also filled mine. We tasted it; it was a bitter, strong wine. It had a particular taste that I did not know, a perfume of vervain and cypress! I drank a few drops, and a profound sadness took possession of my soul. Hippel, on the contrary, clicked his tongue in a satisfied manner.

"Famous," he said, "famous! Where do you get it from, good Mother?"

"From a nearby hill," said the old woman, with a strange smile.

"A famous hill," said Hippel, pouring a new draught. It seemed to me that he was drinking blood.

"What the Devil do you think you're doing, Ludwig," he said to me. "Is something the matter with you?"

"No," I replied, "but I don't like red wine."

"It's necessary not to argue about tastes," observed Hippel, emptying the bottle and thumping the table. "Same again!" he cried. "Always the same, and above all no mixing, lovely hostess! I know better than that. Damn, this wine is reanimating me; it's a generous wine."

Hippel leaned back on the back of his chair. His face appeared to me to decompose. In a single draught I emptied the bottle of white wine; then joy returned to my heart. My friend's preference for the red wine appeared to me to be ridiculous, but excusable.

We continued drinking until one o'clock in the morning, he drinking the red, me the white.

One o'clock in the morning! It is Madame Fantasia's hour of audience. The caprices of the imagination display their diaphanous robes embroidered with crystal and azure, like those of the bluebottle, the beetle and the damsel-fly of dormant waters.

One o'clock! It is then that the celestial music tickles the ear of the dreamer and blows the harmony of invisible spheres into his soul. Then the mouse trots; then the owl deploys its downy wings as it passes silently above our heads; then, too, the vampire extends its pointed muzzle over the artery of its victim and pumps a trickle of blood as thin as the hair of an angel. Its crouching body inflates like a blister and its great wings fall back by its sides, quivering, like those of nocturnal moths.

"One o'clock," I said to my comrade. "It's necessary to get some sleep if we want to leave tomorrow."

Hippel stood up, tottering.

The old woman conducted us to a room with two beds and wished us a pleasant slumber.

We got undressed; I stayed on my feet longer in order to put out the light. I had scarcely lain down when Hippel was profoundly asleep; his respiration resembled the breath of the tempest. I could not close my eyes; a thousand bizarre figures were fluttering around me: gnomes, imps, and the witches of Walpürgisnacht were executing their cabalistic dance on the ceiling. A singular effect of the white wine!

I got up, I lit my lamp and I approached Hippel's bed, drawn by an invincible curiosity. His face was red, his mouth open; blood was making his temples throb. His lips were moving as if he were trying to speak. For a long time I stayed motionless beside him; I would have liked to plunge my gaze into the depths of his soul, but slumber is an impenetrable mystery; like death, it keeps its secrets.

Sometimes Hippel's features expressed terror, sometimes sorrow, sometimes melancholy; sometimes they contracted, and one might have thought that he was about to weep.

That fine face, made for bursting into laughter, had a strange character under the impression of dolor.

What was happening in the depths of that abyss? I could see a few waves rising to the surface, but whence did those profound commotions come?

Suddenly, the sleeper sat up, his eyelids opened, and I saw that his eyes were white. All the muscles of his face quivered; his mouth seemed to want to utter a cry of horror . . . then he fell back and uttered a sob.

"Hippel! Hippel!" I cried, pouring the contents of a jug of water over his head.

He woke up.

"Ah!" he said. "God be praised, it was a dream! My dear Ludwig, I thank you for having woken me up."

"That's all right, but you're going to tell me what you were dreaming."

"Yes . . . tomorrow . . . let me sleep; I'm tired."

"You're an ingrate Hippel! Tomorrow you'll have forgotten everything."

"Damn it," he said, "I'm tired . . . I can't do any more! Let me be . . . let me be."

I did not want to let go. "Hippel, you'll fall back into your dream, and this time, I'll abandon you without mercy."

Those words produced an admirable effect.

"Fall back into my dream!" he cried, leaping out of bed. "Quickly, my clothes! My horse! I'm leaving! This house is accursed. You're right, Ludwig, the Devil lives within these four walls. Let's get out of here!"

He got dressed precipitately. When he had finished I stopped him.

"Hippel," I said, "why run away? It's only three o'clock in the morning; let's repose."

I opened a window; the fresh nocturnal air penetrating into the room dissipated all our dread.

Leaning on the window sill, he recounted the following:

"We were talking yesterday about the famous vineyards of the Rhingau. Although I've never traveled in this country, my mind is doubtless preoccupied by it, and the strong wine we drank gave a somber color to my ideas. The most astonishing thing is that I imagined in my dream that I was the burgomeister of Welche[1]—a nearby hamlet—and I identified so completely with that person that I could make a description of him as of myself. That burgomeister was a man of medium height, almost as fat as me. He wore a coat with long tails and brass buttons; along his legs he had another row of little buttons like the heads of nails. A tricorn hat coiffed his bald head. In sum, he was a man of stupid gravity, only drinking water, only esteeming money, and only thinking about extending his property.

"As I had taken on the burgomeister's coat, I had also taken on his character. As Hippel, I would have been scornful of myself if I had been able to know myself . . . animal of a burgomeister that I was! Isn't it better to live cheerfully and not to care about the future than to pile up coins and distill bile? But there it is . . . I'm a burgomeister.

"I get out of bed and the first thing that worries me is knowing whether the workmen are laboring on the vines. I have a crust of bread for breakfast. A crust of bread! He must be a skinflint, a miser! Me, who breakfasts every day with a good cutlet and an excellent bottle! Anyway, it's all right. I take . . . which is to say the burgomeister takes . . .

1 *Welche* or *Velche* is a pejorative term used by Germans for foreigners in general but particularly the French.

a crust of bread, and puts it in his pocket. He orders his old housekeeper to sweep the room and prepare dinner for eleven o'clock. Broth and potatoes, I think. A poor dinner! No matter . . . he goes out.

"I could make you a description of the house, the road, and the mountain," Hippel told me. "I have them before my eyes.

"Is it possible that a man, in his dreams, can imagine a landscape like that? I saw fields, gardens, meadows, vine-yards. I thought: *that one's Pierre's, that other one's Jacques', that one's Henri's*, and I stopped in front of some of those parcels, saying to myself: *Damn, Jacob's clover is superb*, and further on: *Damn, that arpent of vines would suit me very well*. But in the meantime, I felt a sort of numbness, an indefinable headache.

"I hastened my pace. As it was morning, the sun rose suddenly and the heat became excessive. I followed a little path that climbed through the vines on the slope of the hill. The path petered out behind the ruins of an old castle, and I could see my four arpents further on. I was in a hurry to arrive there. I was out of breath as I penetrated in the midst of the ruins. I stopped in order to get my breath back, but the blood was buzzing in my ears and my heart was thumping in my breast like a hammer on an anvil. The sun was on fire.

"I tried to resume my route, but I was suddenly struck as if by a sledgehammer; I fell down behind a section of wall, and I understood that I had just been afflicted by apoplexy.

"Then a somber despair took possession of me. *I'm dead*, I said to myself; *the money I've amassed with so much difficulty, the trees I've cultivated with so much care, the house I've built—all is lost, all of it will pass to my heirs. Those wretches, to whom I didn't want to give a kreutzer, will enrich themselves at my expense. Oh, traitors, you'll be gladdened by my misfortune . . . you'll take the keys from my pocket, you'll share out my wealth, you'll spend my gold. And I . . . I'll witness that pillage! What a frightful torture!*

"I sensed my soul being detached from the cadaver, but it remained standing beside it.

"That burgomeister's soul saw that its cadaver had a blue face and yellow hands.

"As it was very warm and a sweat of death was trickling over the forehead, large flies came to settle on the face. One of them entered into the nose . . . the cadaver didn't budge! Soon the entire face was covered, and the desolate soul couldn't chase them away!

"It was there . . . there, for minutes that it counted like centuries. Its Hell was commencing!

"An hour went by; the heat was still increasing; not a breath of wind in the air, not a cloud in the sky!

"A goat appeared alongside the ruins; it was browsing the ivy and the wild herbs that grew in the midst of that rubble. As it passed close to my poor corpse it bounded sideways, and then came back, opened its large eyes anxiously, sniffed the surroundings and continued its capricious route along the ledge of a tower. A young pastor who perceived it then ran to pick it up, but on seeing the cadaver he uttered a loud scream and started running as fast as he could toward the village.

"Another hour, as slow as eternity, went by. Finally, whispers and footsteps are heard behind the enclosure and I see climbing up, slowly . . . slowly . . . the justice of the peace, followed by this clerk and several other people. I recognize all of them. They make exclamations at the sight of me. 'It's our burgomeister!'

"The physician approaches my body and chases away the flies, which flutter and swirl like a swarm. He looks, lifts up an arm that is already stiff. Then he says, indifferently: 'Our burgomeister has died of a devastating apoplectic fit; he must have been there since this morning. You can take him away, and have him buried as quickly as possible, for this heat hastens decomposition.'"

"'In truth,' said the clerk, 'it's no great loss to the commune. He was a miser, an imbecile who didn't understand anything about anything.'

"'Yes,' added the judge, 'and he had a very critical expression.'

"'That's not astonishing,' someone else said. 'Fools always believe themselves to be intelligent.'

"'It will be necessary to send for porters,' said the physician. 'Their burden will be heavy; the man had more belly than brain.'

"'I'll draw up the death certificate. What time shall we put on it?' said the clerk.

"'Put that he died at three o'clock.'

"'The miser!' said a peasant. 'He was going to spy on his workers to have a pretext for docking their pay at the end of the week.' Then he folded his arms and looked down at the cadaver. 'Well, burgomeister,' he said, 'what good does it do you now to have pressured the poor people so much? Death has scythed you down just the same.'

"'What's that in his pocket?' said another. He fetched out my crust of bread. 'This is his breakfast!'

"They all burst out laughing.

"Chatting in that fashion, the fellows headed for the exit from the ruins. My poor soul heard them for a few more seconds, and then the sound gradually ceased. I remained in solitude and silence.

"The flies came back in thousands.

"I don't know how much time passed," Hippel went on, "for in my dream, the minutes were endless. However, the porters arrived; they cursed the burgomeister as they lifted my cadaver. The poor man's soul followed them, plunged in an inexpressible dolor. I went back down the same path that I had climbed, but this time I saw my body carried before me on a litter.

"When we arrived at my house I found a crowd of people waiting for me; I recognized my cousins of both sexes, unto the fourth generation!

"The stretcher was set down. They all passed me in review.

"'It's really him.' said one.

"'He's really dead,' said another.

"My housekeeper also arrived, and put her hands together sympathetically. 'Who could have foreseen this misfortune?' she exclaimed. "A big, fat man, so healthy! How little we are!'

"That was my entire funeral oration.

"I was taken inside and laid down on a bed of straw.

"When one of my cousins took the keys from my pocket I tried to utter a cry of rage. Unfortunately, souls have no voice. In sum, my dear Ludwig, I saw my writing-desk opened, my money counted, my credits calculated; I saw the seals put on, I saw my housekeeper stealing my best clothes covertly; and although death had freed me from all needs, I couldn't help regretting the thousandth part of the money that I saw stolen.

"I was undressed and a chemise was put on me; I was nailed between four planks and I witnessed my own funeral.

"When I was lowered into the grave, despair took possession of my soul. All was lost . . . !

"It was then that you woke me up, Ludwig; and I think I can still hear the earth falling over my coffin."

Hippel fell silent and I saw a frisson run through his entire body.

We remained meditative for some time, without exchanging a word. The song of a cock informed us that night was nearing its end; the stars appeared to be fading as daylight approached. Two more cocks launched their piercing voices into space, and responded to one another from farm to farm. A guard dog came out of its niche in order to make its morning round, and then a skylark, doubtless drunk on dew, twittered a few notes of its joyful song.

"Hippel," I said to my comrade, "it's time to go if we want to take advantage of the cool air."

"That's true," he said, "but before anything else, it's necessary to have a bite to eat."

We went downstairs. The innkeeper was in the process of getting dressed. When he had put on his smock he served us the debris of our meal. He filled one of my pitchers with white wine, the other with red wine, saddled our two nags, and wished us bon voyage.

We were not yet half a league from the inn when my friend Hippel, always devoured by thirst, took a mouthful of red wine.

"Brr!" he said, as if struck by vertigo. "My dream, my night's dream!" He urged his horse to a trot in order to escape that vision, which was painted in strange characters on his physiognomy; I followed at a distance, my poor Rosinante, demanding to be spared . . .

Soon the sun rose; a pale rosy tint invaded the somber azure of the sky. The starts were lost in the midst of a dazzling light, like a pearly gravel in the depths of the sea.

With the first rays of the morning, Hippel stopped his horse and waited for me.

"I don't know," he said, "what somber ideas have taken possession of me. That red wine must have some singular virtue; it flatters my throat but attacks my brain."

"Hippel," I responded, "it's necessary not to dissimulate that certain liquors contain the principle of fantasy, and even of phantasmagoria. I've seen cheerful men become sad, sad men become cheerful, intelligent men become stupid and reciprocally with a few glasses of wine in the stomach. It's a profound mystery; what insensate being would dare to doubt that magical power of the bottle? Is it not the scepter of a superior, incomprehensible power, before which we must bow our heads, since everything within us is sometimes submissive to the divine or infernal influence?"

Hippel recognized the force of my arguments, and remained silent, as if lost in an immense reverie.

We were following a narrow path that snaked along the banks of the Quiech. The birds were making their songs heard; grouse were uttering their guttural cries and hiding beneath the broad vine leaves. The landscape was magnificent, the river murmuring as it flowed through little ravines. To the right and the left hills unfurled charged with superb harvests.

Our route formed a bend as it climbed the hillside. Suddenly, my friend Hippel stopped dead, his mouth open, his hands extended in an attitude of stupor; then, as swift as an arrow, he turned to flee, but I grabbed the bridle of his horse.

"What's the matter Hippel?" I exclaimed. "Is Satan lying in ambush before you? Has Balaam's angel made his sword shine in your eyes?"

"Let me be!" he said, struggling. "My dream! It's my dream!"

"Come on, calm down, Hippel. The red wine undoubtedly has harmful properties; take a mouthful of this one, it's a generous juice that drives away somber imaginations from the human brain."

He drank avidly; the beneficent liquor reestablished equilibrium between his faculties.

We poured the red wine, which had become as black as ink, on to the path; it formed large bubbles as it seeped into the ground, and it seemed to me that I heard dull groans, confused voices and sighs, but very faint—so faint that one might have thought that they were escaping from a distant country, and that our ears of flesh couldn't grasp them, but only the most intimate fibers of the heart. It was the last sigh of Abel when his brother felled him in the grass and the earth drank his blood.

Hippel was too emotional to pay attention to that phenomenon, but I was profoundly affected by it. At the same time I saw a black bird as big as a fist emerge from a bush and fly away, uttering a little cry of terror.

"I sense," Hippel said to me then, "that two contrary principles are struggling in my being, the black and the white, the principles of good and evil—let's go!"

We continued our route. "Ludwig," my comrade soon said, "things happen in this world that are so strange that the mind ought to be humiliated and tremulous. You know that I have never traveled in this country. Well, yesterday, I dreamed, and today I see with my eyes the fantasy of the dream looming up before me. Look at this landscape; it's the same one that I saw yesterday in my slumber. Here are the ruins of the old castle where I was struck by apoplexy. Here is the path that I traveled, and over there are my four arpents of vines. There isn't a tree, a stream or a bush that I don't recognize, as if I had seen them a hundred times. When we've gone round this bend in the path, we'll see the hamlet of Welche in the depths of the valley. The second house on the right is the burgomeister's. It has five windows on the upper part of the façade, four and the door on the lower part. To the left of my house—which is to say, the burgomeister's house—you'll see a barn and a stable. It's there that I enclose my livestock. Behind it, in a small yard under a vast stall, is my two-horse press. Finally, my dear Ludwig, such as I am, I'm resuscitated. The poor burgomeister is looking at you through my eyes, speaking to you through my mouth, and if I didn't remember that before I was a burgomeister, a skinflint, a miser and a rich landowner,

I was Hippel, the bon vivant, I'd hesitate to say whom I am, for what I see reminds me of another existence, other habits and other ideas."

Everything happened as Hippel had predicted; we saw the village in the distance, in the depths of a superb valley between two rich hills, the houses scattered along the banks of the river. The second on the right was the burgomeister's.

All the individuals we encountered, Hippel had a vague memory of having known; several of them appeared so familiar to him that he was on the point of calling them by name, but the word remained on his tongue; he could not disengage it from his other memories. In any case, on seeing the indifferent curiosity with which people were looking at us, Hippel sensed clearly that he was unknown and that his face masked the defunct soul of the burgomeister entirely.

We dismounted in front of an inn that my friend identified to me as the best in the village; he had known it for a long time.

A new surprise: the mistress of the inn was a stout woman, widowed for several years, whom the burgomeister had once coveted in a second marriage. Hippel was tempted to throw his arms around her; all his old sympathies awoke simultaneously. However, he was able to moderate himself. The true Hippel combated the matrimonial tendencies of the burgomeister within him. He therefore limited himself to asking, with his most amiable expression, for a good breakfast and the best wine in the place.

When we were at table, a very natural curiosity led Hippel to ask what had happened in the village since his death. "Madame,' he said to our hostess with a flattering smile, "you doubtless knew the former burgomeister of Welche?"

"Do you mean the one who died three years ago of an apoplectic fit?" she asked.

"Precisely," replied my comrade, fixing a furious gaze upon the woman.

"Oh, did I know him!" cried the woman. "That eccentric, that old skinflint who wanted to marry me! If I'd known that he'd die so soon, I'd have accepted. He proposed to me a mutual donation to the last survivor."

That response disconcerted my dear Hippel somewhat . . . the burgomeister's self-esteem was horribly offended within him. However, he contained himself.

"So you didn't love him, Madame?" he said.

"How is it possible to love an ugly, dirty, repulsive, miserly skinflint?"

Hippel stood up in order to look at himself in the mirror. On seeing his cheeks full and plump, he smiled at his face, and came back to take his place before a pullet, which he started to tear apart.

"In fact," he said, "the burgomeister might have been ugly and dirty; that doesn't prove anything against me."

"Are you one of his relatives?' asked the hostess, very surprised.

"Me! I never knew him. I'm only saying that some people are ugly, and others handsome; just because one has a nose placed in the middle of the face, like your burgomeister, it doesn't prove that one resembles him."

"Oh no," said the woman, "you don't have any of his family's features."

"Besides which," said my comrade, "I'm not a miser, myself, which demonstrates that I'm not your burgomeister. Bring us another two bottles of your best wine."

The lady went out, and I seized the opportunity to warn Hippel not to launch into conversations that might betray his incognito.

"What do you take me for, Ludwig?" he cried, furiously. "Know that I'm no more a burgomeister than you are, and the proof is that my papers are in order."

He took out his passport. The hostess came back.

"Madame," he said, "did your burgomeister resemble this description?" He read: "Medium forehead, large nose, thick lips, gray eyes, tall stature, brown hair."

"Very nearly," said the lady, "except that he was bald."

Hippel passed his hand through his hair, crying: "The burgomeister was bald, and no one would dare to sustain that I'm bald."

The hostess thought that my friend was mad, but as he stood up while paying the bill, she said nothing.

When we arrived on the threshold, Hippel turned to me and said in a brusque tone: "Let's go."

"One moment, my dear friend," I replied. "First you're going to take me to the cemetery where the burgomeister is at rest."

At that proposition, his face fell. "No!" he cried. "No, never! You want to precipitate me into the claws of Satan, then? Me, stand on my own grave! That would be contrary to all the laws of nature . . . you can't think so, Ludwig!"

"Calm down, Hippel," I said. "At this moment you're under the empire of invisible powers . . . they're extending their nets over you, so delicate and so transparent that no one can perceive them. It requires an effort to dissolve them; it's necessary to restore the burgomeister's soul, and that's only possible at his tomb. Do you want to be the thief of that poor soul? It would be a manifest theft, and I know your delicacy too well to suppose you capable of such an infamy."

Those invincible arguments convinced him.

"Oh well," he said, "yes, I'll have the courage to trample underfoot those remains, of which I've taken away the heavier half. Please God, let such a theft not be imputed to me. Follow me, Ludwig; I'll take you."

He walked at a rapid, precipitate pace, holding his hat in his hand, his hair scattered, waving his arms, stretching his legs like an unfortunate man accomplishing the final act of despair, and stimulating himself in order not to weaken.

Firstly we traversed several small streets, and then the bridge of a mill, the heavy wheel of which was stirring up a white sheet of foam; then we followed a path that crossed a meadow, and we finally arrived, behind the village, at a rather high wall covered in moss and clematis. It was the cemetery.

In one of the corners the ossuary stood, in the other a neat house surrounded by a small garden.

Hippel launched himself into the room. The gravedigger was there; along the walls there were wreaths of immortelles. The gravedigger was sculpting a cross; this work absorbed him to such an extent that he stood up, frightened, when Hippel appeared. My comrade fixed him with a stare that must have frightened him, because he remained utterly nonplussed for several seconds.

"My worthy man," I said to him, "take us to the grave of the burgomeister."

"There's no need," cried Hippel. "I know it." Without waiting for a response, he opened the door that led to the cemetery and started to run like an insensate, leaping over the graves and shouting: "It's there! There! We have it!" Evidently, the spirit of Evil had possessed him, for as he passed he knocked over a white cross crowned with roses—the cross of a little child!

The gravedigger and I followed him at a distance.

The cemetery was vast. Thick, lush dark green grass rose to three feet above ground. The cypresses dragged their long tresses on the ground, but what struck me immediately was a trellis backed up against the wall and covered with a magnificent vine, so laden with grapes that the clusters were falling on top of one another.

While walking I said to the gravedigger: "You have a vine there that must bring you a good deal."

"Oh, Monsieur," he said, in a plaintive tone, "that vine doesn't bring me anything much. No one wants my grapes; what comes from death returns to death."

I stared at the man. He had a false gaze; a diabolical smile contracted his lips and his cheeks. I didn't believe what he was saying to me.

We arrived at the burgomeister's tomb. It was near the wall. Opposite, there was an enormous vine cep, swollen with juice, which seemed stuffed with it, like a boa constrictor. Its roots doubtless penetrated all the way to the depth of the coffins and disputed their prey with the worms. Furthermore, its grapes were a violet red, while those of the other ceps were a slightly vermilion blue.

Hippel, leaning on the vine, seemed a little calmer.

"You don't eat these grapes," I said to the gravedigger, "but you sell them."

He went pale and made a negative gesture.

"You sell them to the village of Welche, and I can name you the inn at which people drink your wine," I exclaimed. "It's the Fleur-de-lis inn."

The gravedigger trembled in every limb. Hippel wanted to hurl himself at the wretch's throat; it required my intervention to prevent him from tearing the man to pieces.

"Scoundrel," he said, "you've made me drink the essence of your burgomeister. I've lost my personality!"

Suddenly, however, a luminous idea crossed his mind. He turned to the wall and adopted a certain favorite attitude of Flemish painters.

"God be praised!" he said, turning back to me. "I've returned the burgomeister's soul to the earth. I'm relieved of an enormous weight."

The next day we continued on our way; my friend Himmel had recovered his natural gaiety.

REMBRANDT

I

REMBRANDT'S reputation was solidly established by 1646. Magnificent engravings, which he made himself, had popularized his original and fantastic manner in Europe. Each of his productions was a progress in art; the admirable understanding of chiaroscuro, the strange contrast of shadow and light, the nocturnal perspective of which he alone explored the mysterious depths, thus justifying the enthusiasm of his numerous partisans.

It would be difficult to go back to the cause of Rembrandt's genius by following its successive developments. The fact is that the eye of that artist, conformed in a special manner, grasped an object better through the half-tones of the dusk than in the dazzling light of day.

Rembrandt was content in the midst of darkness.

During his youth he was often encountered in the dark taverns where good Flemish heads, grouped around a tale, received the jaundiced and rancid light of a greasy lamp or the gray reflection of a leaded window.

After the death of his wife Rembrandt retired to an old house in the Rue des Juifs in Leyden.[1] His family only consisted then of a sister charged with the cares of the household and a son, a young man of eighteen or twenty, whose character was not yet determined.[2]

The second-hand dealers, always on the lookout for his paintings, had free entry to the painter's house.

One evening in the month of March 1646, Rembrandt, habitually sad and somber, was in a joyful mood. During supper, his verve was reanimated; he made a thousand humorous remarks about his sister Louise, who was, he said, of an age to marry—she was then fifty-five years old. He also praised his son, Christian, and found all sorts of excellent qualities in him that he had not perceived before. Finally, something essentially rare, he sent for a bottle of old porter, and took several swigs therefrom.

When ten o'clock chimed and the watchman had uttered his lugubrious cry in the midst of the silence, Rembrandt lit a lamp and went out, wishing Louise and his son good night.

---

1 I have left this street name as the authors render it. In fact, in 1846 Rembrandt van Rijn lived in what was then called Breestraat [Broad Street], which later became known as Jodenbreestraat because it became the heart of the Jewish quarter—hence the authors' improvisation.

2 Rembrandt's wife Saskia died in 1642, shortly after the birth of their only surviving child, Titus; the one featured in the story is fictitious, as is the sister. The historical Rembrandt then had a relationship with the nurse he had hired to took after his dying wife, who subsequently sued him for breach of promise, whereupon he began a relationship with his maid, who was banned from received communion in consequence.

They heard him traverse the vestibule and open the studio door. He went in.

That high-ceilinged room received daylight through a single window, which rose up from the floor all the way to the vault. A red silk curtain intercepted the light; it could be drawn back and forth by means of a slide. Old suits of armor were suspended from the wall, with helmets, axes and daggers covered with an inveterate rust; Rembrandt, careless of the traditions of Greece and Italy, called them his antiques.

In front of the window, on his easel, reposed a painting of medium size. The artist advanced a chair and sat down, projecting a light on that newly-panted canvas. It was *The Sacrifice of Abraham*, one of his masterpieces, now the ornament of the museum of Saint Petersburg.[1]

In the presence of his work, the vulgar face of the painter lit up with a reflection of genius.

"It's beautiful," he said, with a proud smile; but then enthusiasm gave way to analysis; his thick eyebrows came together and he started examining the details of the work. Sometimes an exclamation of pleasure escaped him, often a gesture of chagrin; he took up his palette convulsively, approached the brush to the canvas and then threw it away. Inarticulate words betrayed the artist's doubts. The execution did not reach the height of his standard.

In the meantime, another figure, no less gripping and no less enthusiastic, no less sublime in inspiration and genius, leaned over Rembrandt's shoulder and looked at the painting avidly.

---

1 *The Sacrifice of Abraham* was actually painted in 1635, but is indeed in the Hermitage Museum in Saint Petersburg.

It was the figure of an old Jew, such as the Flemish painter has transmitted to us several times. Imagine a long, thin, bony body enveloped in a kind of green robe with large checks, shoes deformed by large silver buckles protruding from beneath the robe and arched legs showing their knotty kneecaps; finally, above all that, a jaundiced head coiffed in a pointed bonnet and furrowed by so many wrinkles that one might have thought it a parchment face of an old Egyptian mummy, the skin stuck to the bald head and cheekbones shining like ivory. A long nose, receding lips, and a prominent, angular chin completed that strange physiognomy, but what gave it an expression of truly inconceivable intelligence was the gaze of large gray eyes, like those of a lynx, darting flashes through the white eyebrows, which almost descended over the eyeballs.

That individual had opened the door with so much prudence that it yielded without the slightest sound; he had advanced behind the painter's stool with such a furtive tread that Rembrandt did not hear him.

Thus, there was the strange spectacle of those two figures in contemplation before the same work. In the features of one the pride of creation was legible, but also the severe self-criticism of the artist; on the face of the other there was surprise, limitless astonishment and enthusiasm at its highest expression.

The one who admired more was the Jew. He had adoration in his pose, his gesture and his gaze.

Suddenly, Rembrandt seized the brush and leaned over the canvas, saying: "That detail spoils the ensemble; it's necessary to change it."

But the Jew, moved by an invincible force, retained the painter's hand.

"No, no!" he cried. "Don't retouch it! I tell you that it's good!"

Frightened by that sudden apparition, Rembrandt turned round with an exclamation of surprise; then, recognizing the dealer in second-hand gods and curios Jonas, he burst out laughing.

"Aha!" he said, "it's you, friend. How the devil did you get in here?"

Without answering the question, the old Jew cried: "Master Rembrandt, this is your masterpiece. It's magnificent, it's sublime! Oh, the God of Israel made a great miracle in saving Abraham's son, but this admirable painting is even more marvelous. You've never attained such perfection."

"Bah!" replied the artist, joyfully. "You always repeat the same thing. According to you, my latest painting is always my masterpiece."

"That's true," said the old man. "That's true, Master Rembrandt; you surpass yourself every time, but you won't go any further."

"Between us, Jonas," said the painter, with a triumphant smile, "you don't know your métier. Instead of criticizing my work, you praise it so highly that . . ."

"To depreciate that painting," the merchant interrupted, "it would be necessary to have lost one's eyes, it would be necessary to be an infamous calumniator. And then, Master, do you not know its value as well as I do?"

"Yes," said Rembrandt, with a hint of conceit, "I'm quite content with this work, and if it weren't sold . . ."

"It's sold!" cried the Jew, in a heart-rending tone. "Sold! But . . . but . . . that's impossible . . . you're joking . . . sold . . . to whom?"

"To a rich German collector. The price was fixed in advance."

"The price was fixed!" repeated the Jew, in consternation. "But what price, Master?"

"A thousand ducats."

"Oh, you're losing your head. What is a thousand ducats for such a work? You'll never do better . . . perhaps even as well . . ."

The painter's face expressed doubt.

"Yes," said the merchant. "I'll offer you fifteen hundred myself."

"Impossible," said the other, regretfully.

"Two thousand!" cried the Jew.

"It's an unfortunate affair, impossible to go back on it," replied Rembrandt. His voice was tremulous, because he liked money.

"Two thousand five hundred ducats!" said the old man. He let himself fall into a chair, as if frightened himself by that exorbitant offer.

Rembrandt fixed him with a penetrating gaze. "It's too much, Jonas," he said. "You'd lose by it."

"Yes, yes, I'm ruining myself," cried the Jew. "I know that, but how can I let such a magnificent painting go to someone else?"

After a momentary silence, the merchant added: "Master Rembrandt, I've promised to deliver to a rich art-lover the first work to emerge from your studio. My word is engaged."

"And I also have my word," said Rembrandt, standing up, but visibly affected. "In any case, the contact is signed."

The Jew stood up and came to take the artist's hand. "Master, master," he said, with a tremor in his voice impossible to describe, "I can't offer you any more. I have a daughter, Master Rembrandt; you know my little Rebecca? If I had no child I'd offer you more. Two thousand five hundred ducats is a great deal . . . it's a magnificent offer, but one never pays too dear for a masterpiece. Come on, how much do you want? Two thousand five hundred ducats, isn't that enough? Can't we reach agreement?"

Those words, pronounced with a surprising volubility, betrayed a keen emotion in the Jew. There was so much trouble and anxiety in his gaze that the artist was touched by it.

"Jonas," he said, showing him the imprint of a seal on the canvas, "this painting is sold, the contract has been doubly signed.

"Well, let the will of God be done," said the Jew, in a penetrating tone. "I'll come back tomorrow to see your collector, and if he's prepared to cede his bargain to me, I'll offer him the difference between our prices."

"That won't get you anywhere," said Rembrandt, "for the acquirer of this painting is the Prince of Hesse-Cassel.[1] You'll be more fortunate another time, Jonas. Believe that I'm afflicted by your setback; I'm losing fifteen hundred ducats in consequence. For a poor artist like me, the father of a family, that's enormous."

---

1 Presumably William VI, Landgrave of Hesse-Kassel from 1637 to 1663; born in 1629 he had not yet reached the age of majority in 1646, but he subsequently became an important patron of the arts.

They both went out, uttering deep sighs. The painter and the Jew were consternated.

Rembrandt escorted Jonas to the threshold of the house.

"By the way," he said, "how did you get into my studio? I didn't hear you."

"Your sister told me where you were."

"Good, good," said the painter, shaking the merchant's hand.

They separated. Eleven o'clock chimed at the cathedral.

Rembrandt traversed a small courtyard that preceded his house. The moon was shining in the sky, pale and meditative. He followed Jonas with his gaze through the tenebrous streets, and then closed the two battens of the coaching entrance, fitted the bar, released two enormous bulldogs into the courtyard, and went back inside, sad and somber.

Rembrandt the miser, Rembrandt the usurer, was losing fifteen hundred ducats!

II

In those days the city of Leyden possessed an establishment remarkable in its genre, the Tavern of the Free Mercenaries.

It was there that children of good families completed their education; it was there that they learned to drink ale and porter, to play cards and dice, and to formulate a *Gotferdum* in an appropriate manner. But also, what a magnificent tavern!

It was not one of those poor hovels where the voices of the drinkers break on the angle of a wall or are crushed beneath a ceiling. One did not see chairs, tables and Argand lamps there, miserable utensils that do not resist the battles of a joyous society. No! The Tavern of the Free Mercenaries was an immense cellar; its vaults, thirty feet high, provided a chorus for Bacchic songs, and never failed to repeat the refrain.

By virtue of a judicious prevision of Madame Catherine, the mistress of the house, ewers served as chairs, barrels as tables, and their solid construction stood up to all species of attack.

Now, on the same night that Master Rembrandt closed his door with so much care and released the bulldogs into the courtyard, Christian, the amiable young man whom he had been praising, was at the Tavern of the Free Mercenaries.

It was very late; the tavern was almost deserted. Only one group of drinkers still remained around a vast barrel. A lamp placed in the middle caused the black silhouettes of the various individuals to stand out against a red background.

All those faces expressed the keenest attention.

Christian, sitting in the front rank, seemed very emotional. Facing him was a lanky fellow whose gaze was glittering with malignity; a long rapier crossed his legs; with one hand he was lifting a leather dice-cup, and in the other a large plumed hat. It appeared that he and Rembrandt's son were at odds; they were playing an infernal game, and Christian was losing.

"Seven," he said, throwing the dice on to the barrel.

All the spectators leaned forward to see the coup.

"Nine," cried the other.

A great silence followed those words; the dice could be heard rattling in the cup.

"Ten!" said Christian.

"Twelve!" cried his adversary.

There was a lively agitation. Christian threw the goblet to the floor and cursed fate.

"Well," said the other, "your word is engaged for twenty-five ducats."

"Are you afraid?" said the young man, angrily.

"No, no, I know you'll pay."

"Of course!" cried a fat Fleming with a beetroot nose. "Of course he'll pay. Dear Christian always pays. He paid yesterday, he'll pay today and he'll pay tomorrow. He breaks the bank as a matter of habit."

Everyone burst out laughing.

"Van Hopp," cried the young man, "you give the impression of mocking me."

"I'm not mocking anyone . . . but I'm saying that you're bankrupt."

"And you," retorted Christian, exasperated, "are too miserly to risk a double! I challenge you!"

"That's possible, my lad. Before playing I like to see the money on the barrel, and you don't have an escalin in your pocket."

Those words, pronounced in a mocking tone, excited Christian's fury to the highest degree, but he contained himself.

"Wait for me, Van Hopp," he said. "You want to see money on the table, you'll see it. And you, Master Van Eick, you'll be paid right away."

He went out precipitately.

All the drinkers sat down around a barrel and relit their pipes, while awaiting the return of Rembrandt's son.

"Hey, Dame Catherine," shouted Christian's adversary. "A moos; I'm paying."

The lady ran and deposited a pitcher on the barrel. The glasses were filled. Van Eick put his arm around Catherine's robust waist and imprinted a vigorous kiss in her cleavage. She let him do it; he had money.

Clouds of smoke rose up above the drinkers. All those gross fleshy faces expressed quietude, the supreme well-being that results from the enjoyment of material life. Not a word or a glance was exchanged; the silence lasted for more than a quarter of an hour.

Finally, Van Hopp's large pipe went out. He emptied it methodically, and said: "Do you know, I don't understand Master Rembrandt; one can't deny that he's a great painter, and even a man full of common sense, but he lavishes money on his son like a madman. It's inconceivable."

"Yes," said another, blowing out a puff of tobacco smoke. "Yes, it's inconceivable."

A further silence.

After a few seconds, Van Hopp said: "It's quite inconceivable."

A third then said: "Christian has lost more than three hundred ducats this week. Master Rembrandt must be blind not to see that his son is an imbecile."

"Bah!" said Van Eick, with a caustic smile. "The young man is in the process of forming himself. A few more lessons, and I promise you to make something presentable of him. His father has understood that, etc. . . ."

"His father," Van Hopp interjected, "is a miser, and I'm sure he doesn't give him an escalin."

At that moment the door opened and Christian appeared, making a long bag full of ducats resonate with a triumphant expression.

"Well, friends," he said, "are you ready?"

He approached Van Eick and threw him a handful of gold. "That's your settlement. And you, Van Hopp, since you want to see money on the barrel . . . there it is. How much are you putting up?"

"All that I have on me," said the Fleming.

They sat down.

By the soul of Satan, the power of gambling is an infernal one. It makes our muscles quiver, our temples throb, our entrails shudder. Fear, joy, triumph, despair, terror and hatred: all the passions are summarized in gambling; all are at its orders.

Gambling, oh, gambling! It would reanimate a cadaver in its tomb; the skeleton of the gambler would seize a dice-cup; its empty eyes would flash, rage would make its teeth grate.

See those apathetic, immobile faces, those stupid gazes, that soft flesh, devoid of sinews and fibers, how everything moves, agitates, twists, contracts, relaxes! Those men are not playing . . . they are watching play; they are not actors in the drama, they are judges, and yet the passion dominates them, grips them in its circle of iron.

An hour later, Christian's ducats had passed into Van Hopp's pocket.

III

Christian left the tavern singing a lewd ditty; the poor fellow did not want to betray his chagrin. As soon as he was in the street, however, a horrible imprecation escaped his breast.

"May the five hundred thousand devils hold you in their claws," he cried, turning to look at the door.

He seized his velvet toque as if to tear it to pieces, but he replaced it on his head and uttered a burst of laughter.

"Bah!" he said. "What's money? Ten, twenty forty ducats? Trivia, nothing at all. Doesn't Jonas offer me his purse? Can't I put my hand in it when it pleases me? Oh, the worthy and honest Jew! I respect you, Jonas, I venerate you! By the God of Israel, I'll have myself circumcised in order to marry your little Rebecca!"

Then Christian launched forth through the deserted streets. Doubtless a luminous idea had just crossed his mind.

The night was dark, the silence as profound as the darkness; rare stars scintillated in the sky through the swell of the clouds, like the phosphorescent gleams that spring from the impact of waves. He went along a canal, the muddy waters of which reflected the black and menacing sky. Rembrandt's son recalled his father's engravings.

Finally, at the corner of the cathedral, where two o'clock was chiming, he stopped in front of an old house and raised his eyes. It was one of those antique constructions dating from the Middle Ages; the gable overhung the street, and little beams, symmetrically disposed, entered into the thickness of the walls. A vast garden extended behind it.

Christian climbed over the wall and made a signal. A few minutes later, a small window opened.

"Is that you, sire?" asked a quavering voice.

"Yes, Esther, it's me."

"Good, good, I recognize you."

A key grated in the lock, the door ceded before a fleshless hand.

"Ah, Sire Rembrandt," said the old woman. "You've been awaited for a long time. Poor little Rebecca no longer hoped to see you . . . she's all in tears."

Christian went upstairs. Esther followed him slowly.

Old Esther was a good woman; she had been serving Jonas for half a century; she loved little Rebecca so much that her slightest caprice was obeyed. Physically, Esther resembled the sibyl of Cumae: small, stooped, wizened, her head nodding, her eyes round and sharp; her mouth had disappeared, since when the old woman's chin and nose formed a beak.

Christian went along a vast corridor, opened a fur-padded door precipitately and arrived in Rebecca's bedroom.

All that our modern luxury has of the sumptuous and rich faded before the splendor of that little apartment. Imagine a high, narrow room with an ogival vault, the ledges decorated with brilliant paintings; from the middle of the vaults a silver chain descends, which retains a bronze candelabrum. An Indian carpet with a thousand capricious rose-designs covers the parquet. Two high windows in the Gothic style, with their bronze mesh and their colored glass, reflect a dazzling light.

Finally, on a soft divan, little Rebecca is reposing.

Oh, Christian, Christian! Fortunate young man!

The daughter of Jonas, a veritable pearl of the Orient, of an ideal purity, was waiting for Rembrandt's son. With her elbow on the edge of the sofa, her head in her hand, her hair scattered over her white shoulders, her moist lips, her voluptuous nostrils, the poor child seemed sad and dejected. A tear was scintillating in her long eyelashes. The ingrate hadn't come!

When he irrupted into the room she could not retain a cry of joy.

"It's you, my friend! Oh, how glad I am! So you haven't forgotten me!"

The young man, on his knees beside her, put his arms around her slender waist, her palpitating bosom and her bare shoulders. Their gazes, their breath and their hair were confounded.

"Oh, how beautiful you are!" he exclaimed. "How beautiful you are!"

Esther entered almost immediately and said: "Life is short, the hours, the months and the years pass by! Old age arrives . . . amuse yourselves, my children . . . be happy!"

An hour went by. The young lovers did not count the minutes. They spoke in low voices, so low that the silence was hardly troubled by them.

Suddenly, the old cathedral clock chimed, and its solemn vibrations were prolonged in the distance. At the same time a door opened at the extremity of the vestibule. Christian shivered and lent an ear.

Slow footsteps approached the room. The young man launched himself toward the candelabrum and snuffed out the lights.

Someone stopped outside the door; a ray of light slid through the lock and formed a star on the wall. Several seconds went by. Christian held his breath. Finally, the footfalls continued along the corridor, the luminous dot described an undulating curve over the wall-hangings, and the sound of footsteps died away.

"What's that?" the young man asked, in a whisper.

"It's my father," said Rebecca. "He walks at night."

Attracted by a fatal curiosity, Rembrandt's son opened the door slightly and looked out. In the distance he saw Jonas, enveloped in a large cloak. His thin arm, holding a torch, emerged like a stem from the folds of his overcoat, and the immense shadow of the old man was projected in the corridor. Having arrived at an oak door he opened it and disappeared.

That apparition had something strange about it.

"What is your father doing at this hour?" Christian asked the young woman.

"I don't know," she replied. "I was still a child when I heard him for the first time. Then I trembled, huddled in a corner and murmured a prayer. Every time, as today, he stops at the door . . . and then his footsteps die away in the distance."

"That's odd," said Christian, a sudden pallor spreading over his face. "He never comes in?" he asked Rebecca.

"No, never."

"What's behind that big oak door?"

"I don't know. He has sole guard of the key. No one goes in there except my father."

"That's surprising," said the young man, increasingly agitated.

"Undoubtedly, my friend. But why worry about something one can't fathom? Come on, let's talk about our amour again."

"I have to go," said Christian. "Your father might know . . ."

"No, no, he doesn't know anything. Stay, I beg you."

She tried to retain him with caresses, but the brave Christian was afraid. He seized his hat, slipped into the vestibule and traversed the garden.

A few minutes later he launched himself into the street at a run, as if he had the Devil at his heels.

IV

The next day, the Prince of Hesse-Cassel, to do honor to the painting, deigned to present himself at Rembrandt's house.

The prince was a superb man; merely by seeing his corkscrew moustache, his hat with white plumes, his embroidered velvet coat, his sword with a golden hilt, his imposing stride and his magnificent gaze, it was necessary to recognize in him one of those superior beings predestined by their ancient nobility and the purity of their blood to govern peoples.

Thus, equitable nature had put him at the head of a principality.

Rembrandt came to receive him on the threshold, in a coat of coarse blue cloth, with a Flemish felt hat and the vulgar face that is familiar to you.

The prince's carriage had stopped in the street.

A steward clad in black ratiné, as thin as a rake, his spine curved, his cheeks pale and hollow, his gaze oblique, his noise pointed and his mouth smiling, followed the prince. When Rembrandt perceived him, holding a long bag of ducats in his hand, the sight gave him pleasure.

"Well, Master," said the prince, "we have come in person to take away your magnificent painting, *The Sacrifice of Abraham*. It's a conquest worthy of us."

"Milord," said the painter, with a caustic glance, "against a mule laden with gold, there is no fortress stronger than yours."

"Ha ha! You take our steward for a quadruped, then?"

"I was talking about the bag," said Rembrandt. "The animal is only an accessory."

The steward grimaced.

"Damn, Rembrandt, you're wicked," said the prince. "Defend yourself, Master Genodet."

"Milord," replied the other, "I would not permit myself to speak before you."

I believe it, thought the artist. *He prefers to take his coin in silence.*

With that, they went into the studio.

In order to manage the effect of his painting, Rembrandt had hung it from the wall in a favorable daylight; he had also covered it with a green cloth, counting on enjoying the prince's surprise when he removed it.

"Would you care to stand here, Milord," he said. "The painting is there; I'll uncover it."

With a noble deference, the Prince of Hesse-Cassel took the position indicated. Then Rembrandt, full of ardor, removed the cloth. But—consternation!—the painting had disappeared.

Milord thought it was a trick.

For a moment, Rembrandt thought he had lost his mind; he put his hands to his head and stood there, struck with stupor. Then he started running around the room like an insensate, searching, bumping into things, knocking things over, crying: "My painting! Where is my painting?"

"Master Rembrandt," exclaimed the prince, "are you playing a comedy? I'm not your dupe!"

An infernal smile creased the steward's lips.

That sight and those words raised the painter's fury to the highest degree.

"A comedy!" he cried. "Me, play a comedy! But I've been robbed! Pillaged! Me, make dupes!"

His cries were such that Louise and Christian came running, fearfully. Then he launched himself toward them shouting: "Is it you? Is it you who has taken my painting?" He grabbed Christian by the collar.

"What painting?" his son asked.

"Oh! It's you . . . there's only you in the house! Come on, Christian, you wanted to play a practical joke, didn't you? I forgive you—but tell me where it is immediately."

"I swear to you, Father, that you're in error . . . ."

"Oh, wretch, you're denying it!"

He was about to strike him when Louise intervened. "My brother!" she cried. "You know that he's incapable of it."

"You're defending him! It was you, then?"

"Me?" said the poor woman, with tears in her eyes. "Oh, Rembrandt, you can't think so!"

The painter fell into a chair without adding another word. He was devastated.

"Let's go," said the prince, with a superb gesture. "This scene is ignoble, it has doubtless been prepared in some tavern. The painting is sold! I'm sorry to have soiled my boots in the home of such rabble."

He went out with as majestic stride; the steward followed him at a trot.

A few seconds later, the prince's carriage was burning the pavement of the Rue des Juifs.

V

The sudden, incomprehensible disappearance of his painting threw Rembrandt into a somber despair.

He was unable to resume work for a long time. At table, he scanned Louise and Christian with a gaze full of suspicion, and only opened his mouth to complain about traitors and ingrates.

"Yes," he said, "one believes that one has a son and a devoted sister. One abandons oneself to them! Well, they are our greatest enemies. Who can one trust? The honest man is the prey of rogues and thieves. His own family exploits him and robs him; his confidence even turns against himself."

Poor Louise remained silent. What response can one make to an unfortunate man eaten away by suspicion?

Sometimes, Rembrandt, pursued by an unspeakable terror, went upstairs and downstairs, running around the corners of his house a hundred times over, like a veritable insensate. He was often seen in the courtyard too, marching with a slow and grave stride, his head bowed, his arms folded over his breast, murmuring unintelligible words.

When his dogs ran to him, heads lowered submissively, wagging their tails with pleasure, he said: "Back! You're traitors too! My thief doubtless fed you, and you caressed his hand like mine."

At eight o'clock in the evening Rembrandt locked his courtyard, fitted the bar, sent Christian and Louise away . . . and then, with a long rapier in his hand, he lay in ambush behind his door until sleep came to close his eyes; then he retired, cursing the weakness of his will, which could not vanquish nature.

In spite of his terrors, however, which touched madness, Rembrandt resumed work after a few days. He even finished the admirable painting of the *Philosopher in Meditation*, imprinted with a melancholy so profound and a sadness so true.[1]

---

1 The painting in question is signed and dated 1632; it surfaced in France in the mid-eighteenth century, ultimately ending up in the Louvre, where it was much admired by the members of the Romantic Movement, being cited by Théophile Gautier and George Sand, among others.

One evening, several blows of the knocker resounded on the door to the courtyard; the painter went out and asked who was knocking.

"It's me, Master Rembrandt," replied the voice of Jonas. "Why the Devil have you locked up so early? I have a few words to say to you."

Rembrandt opened a judas-hole pierced in the door. "Well, say them!" he exclaimed, in a surly tone.

The face of the dealer appeared, with its thousand wrinkles and tanned skin. "Master," he said, "do you not have a painting to sell? An art-lover has presented himself."

"Bring him tomorrow," said the artist. "I've just completed a work of fantasy."

"The man addressed himself to me," said Jonas, "and you can imagine . . ."

"Yes, I can imagine! You need a commission. Henceforth, I'll handle my affairs myself."

He closed the judas-hole and went inside.

It was thus that poor Jonas was dismissed, for the painter's humor, scarcely agreeable by habit, was further embittered.

Although he could not work in the evening by lamplight, he rarely left his studio. The neighbors even perceived a light in that room all night long, and a shadow was often cut out on the large curtain of red silk.

What was Rembrandt doing at that hour when profound sleep resembles death, when silence reigns far and wide in the deserted streets, when green eyes of cats light up with an interior glow, as if they were carrying torches in their heads? At the hour when a young woman sees

in her dreams a handsome young man of the neighbor-
hood on his knees before her, one of his hands over his
trembling lips, and she says to him softly: "Alfred"—or
Charles, or Jules—"I love you, yes, I want to be yours!"

At that sinister or benevolent hour, Rembrandt is
awake. He lifts up a heavy trapdoor in the middle of his
studio and goes down a few steps. A feverish agitation
makes his muscles shudder, and flashes escape his gaze;
he plunges his arms into a profound cavity and brings
out, effortfully, an iron coffer. He blushes with joy, a
Satanic smile expands his broad face . . . he lifts the lid
and gazes. Rembrandt the miser cannot say a word; his
emotion suffocates him, his hands bathe in the gold, he
stammers with a little staccato cry: "Ho . . . ho . . . ho!
Laugh, my children, laugh! My poor little angels . . . ho
. . . ho . . . ho . . . how happy they are! How they sing . . .
my little angels!"

While pronouncing those insensate words, the miser
agitates his ducats and makes them stream; they render a
heavy and dull sound, for he has a great deal of gold; the
coffer is full of it.

But suddenly, Rembrandt's face is decomposed; his
eyes dilate . . . his neck cranes . . . his mouth partly open,
fear painted on his features . . .

He listened . . .

A little sound was audible in the vestibule . . . as if
the floorboards of the stairwell were flexing under a rapid
step.

Gently, very gently, the miser slid the coffer into the
depths of the cellar and closed the trapdoor again. Then,
courage returning to him, he bounded toward a dagger

suspended from the wall, and like a tiger emerging from its cage he launched himself into the vestibule, shouting: "I have the wretch!"

At that moment, a shadow glided across the top of the staircase and disappeared, as if by enchantment.

Rembrandt was stupefied. But a sudden thought crossed his mind; he ran to the room where his new painting was . . . he darted a glance at the wall . . . only the location and the nail remained!

Louise, awakened with a start, heard a cry that no human breast has ever extracted from the depths of its entrails. The poor woman trembled; a cold sweat extended over her limbs. She had recognized her brother's voice!

After that unique, sinister cry, the silence became imposing . . . terrible!

In spite of her fear, she had the courage to get up and run to Rembrandt's room.

The painter, backed up against the wall, pale and livid, his fists clenched, his legs braced, foaming at the mouth, his eyes open but devoid of a gaze, seemed annihilated. One might have thought that he was an upright cadaver.

Louise tried to speak, but no sound succeeded in emerging from her mouth; her tongue was chilled by terror. She had to support herself in order not to fall.

Gradually, Rembrandt came round. He made a gesture, and then uttered a long sigh. Life was reanimated, at the same time as fury.

"I've been robbed! Robbed!" he said.

"Brother!" cried Louise. "Brother!"

He looked at her coldly. "It's you," he said. "You were there?"

"I've come running . . ."

"And Christian?"

"He's asleep, Brother."

"He's asleep . . . we'll go and see."

Rembrandt headed for his son's room. Louise followed him.

"Christian!" he cried, opening the door.

No response. He opened the alcove and looked. The bed was empty.

He tore away the pillow, the sheets, overturned everything. He could not render to the evidence, but doubt was no longer possible. A sinister smile brushed the painter's lips

"That's all right," he said, in a curt and concentrated voice; "now I know my thief!"

Louise dissolved in tears.

VI

Christian had spent the night at the Tavern of the Free Mercenaries. At four o'clock in the morning, when the first tints of daylight were blanching the chimney-pots, our brave young man, a little drunk, was strolling tranquilly along the Rue des Juifs. He stopped in front of Rembrandt's courtyard and introduced a skeleton key into the lock. He waited, as usual, to see the two dogs, his accomplices, run to him joyfully. He was astonished, therefore, when a heavy and muscular hand fell upon the collar of his tunic and his father's voice cried: "Wretch! I've got you!"

He was dragged into the house with such rapidity that he did not have time to fall to his knees and beg for mercy.

In the middle of the studio, Rembrandt and his son looked one another in the face, Christian red-faced, with fear in his stomach, Rembrandt pale, his eyes glittering, with rage in his heart.

For a few seconds the painter remained silent. The young man felt a sort of frisson climb along his spine.

"Father," he cried, "I'm a great culpable . . . make reproaches to me, I've merited them all!"

"My painting," Rembrandt interjected, in a dry voice.

Christian saw that fine phrases were not in season, for Master Rembrandt was holding an enormous stick, and did not appear to be joking.

"My two paintings," he repeated, in a staccato tone. "Speak, thief, where have you put them?"

"I don't have them, Father," said Christian, putting his hands together.

"Where are you coming from?"

"I'm coming . . . I'm coming . . . from the tavern."

"Ah! You're coming from the tavern," said Rembrandt, with a bitter smile. "And you eat, drink and gamble at the tavern don't you, wretch?"

No response.

"You have nothing to say. You eat, you drink, you gamble, that's agreed. Who gives you the money?"

Christian hesitated.

"Who gives you the money?" Rembrandt howled. "Speak, rogue, or I'll crush you." He lifted the large stick, and Christian felt the flesh of his back shiver with horror; but the painter lowered his arm, and said: "I know where you get the money . . . it's you who stole my paintings, in order to sell them."

"I don't steal, Father, I borrow."

"You borrow!" cried Rembrandt, with a new fury. "You borrow! From whom, and how much, wretch?"

Frightened, Christian replied: "Jonas lends me the money."

"Jonas! A Jew, a usurer! He lends to you? How much . . . how much?"

"The poor fellow dared not say everything; he only admitted half the sum: five hundred ducats.

Scarcely had he pronounced the words than Rembrandt launched such a blow of the stick that the unfortunate fell to the floor, crying like a damned soul: "I'm dead!"

But Rembrandt, pitiless, seized him rudely and dragged him into a nearby room, which had only a single grilled window.

"Wretch," he said to him, "if you don't tell me where my paintings are, you'll die of starvation."

He went out immediately, and locked the door with a double turn.

Christian, his back bruised, remained alone in that narrow, dark room, with no other perspective than fasting for a long time. A singular contrast with the Tavern of the Free Mercenaries!

When Rembrandt returned to the vestibule he encountered Louise. The poor woman's eyes were very red, her bonnet was askew, her chemisette loose; in sum, she was a pitiful sight.

Rembrandt looked at her as a wild boar looks at a dog.

"What do you want?" he said.

"Brother, that unfortunate child doesn't know. . . ."

"Listen, Mademoiselle," the painter interjected, "I forbid you to criticize my actions, or I'll throw you out."

"I'm not criticizing, Brother, I'm only saying . . ."

"You have nothing to say!" he cried, furiously. "Occupy yourself with the housework."

Louise withdrew, trembling. She swallowed her tears.

When mealtime came, she informed her brother.

"I'm not eating," he said.

"And Christian?"

"The wretch isn't eating either," said Rembrandt.

"Nor me," said Louise, retiring.

That evening, a remarkable scene occurred.

Christian had the hunger of a cannibal, and Rembrandt too, but he was obstinate in not eating. Christian started to howl that he was hungry. Then his father, approaching the door, said to him: "Where are my paintings?"

"I'm hungry! I'm hungry!" was the son's only response.

"So am I," murmured Rembrandt, in a low voice. "I'm hungry too. What he's suffering, I know." He placed his hands on his breast.

At ten o'clock Louise came to announce supper.

"I'm not eating," said Rembrandt—but as he pronounced the words he turned toward the kitchen and inhaled the odor of roast meat. Louise persisted.

"I tell you that I'm not hungry! Close that door; the odor inconveniences me."

"And him?" Louise asked

"Him!" cried the painter. "Let him tell me where my paintings are, and I'll forgive him."

He pronounced those words in a loud voice, in order that his son could hear them. But for all response, Christian kicked the door from time to time, shouting: "I'm hungry!"

"Too bad," said Rembrandt. "He's obstinate, I'll be obstinate. We'll see which of us gives in."

In spite of his anger, the painter wanted to undergo the torture that he was imposing on Christian. The father was suffering, but the miser made the law!

VII

A strange agitation reigned in Jonas' house.

Rebecca had waited for Christian until very late; the young man had not come and the girl had gone to bed in tears.

For several days she had been experiencing an indefinable malaise: constrictions of the heart, stomach cramps and dizzy spells; she uttered long sighs. Only the presence of the young man could give her a momentary calm, but after his departure she wept, lamented and could not sleep. Those symptoms announced an extraordinary and dangerous malady.

That day, Christian having neglected his visit, the symptoms took on alarming proportions. When old

Esther came into her young mistress's room in the morning she found her pale and dejected; her forehead was burning, she was yawning, sighing and moaning.

"Oh, my God," she said, "my God have pity on me; I'm going to die."

"Die!" cried Esther. "Die! Oh, don't say such things, my child."

"Yes, yes, I'm ill . . . I'm suffering here!" She placed her white hand on her epigastrum. "I'm suffocating . . . I can't take any moiré."

Frightened, Esther hastened to warn Jonas. The latter came running.

At the sight of his daughter, hearing her plaints and seeing her eyes filled with tears, a terrible fear took possession of the old man.

He invoked the God of Abraham and Jacob.

"Oh, my poor little Rebecca!" he cried. "My child, my treasure, are you ill? Tell me. You've doubtless been exposed to a draught, you've committed some great imprudence. Speak, don't hide anything from me."

For her only response, the poor child agitated her arms, bowed her charming head with languor, and large tears, as brilliant as morning dew, scintillated under her long eyelids.

Then the desperate Jones ran out of the house, while old Esther prepared a calming, emollient and refreshing tisane.

A few minutes later Jonas reappeared with Doctor Jerosonimo.

Picture a man between seventy and eighty years old, as thin and stiff as a pole. He is dressed in a long green silk toga; the twelve signs of the zodiac are represented on a large border of red silk, and all the constellations, embroidered in silver, stand out on that mantle of sorts. Furthermore, a great pointed bonnet rises perpendicularly on the doctor's head; a long white beard, similarly pointed, descends over his stomach; spectacles of fabulous grandeur repose on the tip of his thin, tapering nose. The doctor gazes over his spectacles, and his little dark eyes dart a ray that lunges into the coverts of your heart. Under his arm he carries a rosewood box encrusted with gold, a veritable ambulant pharmacy. Finally, the individual's manner is severe, his gesture imposing and his speech sententious.

He deposited his magnificent box on a marble table and opened it. Then, in a quantity of little compartments, sachets and phials became visible: elixirs, opiates and electuaries in a thousand different colors.

It was beautiful, and at the sight of that arsenal directed against all maladies, everyone had to understand that Doctor Jerosonimo was a well—a cistern, an abyss—of science

"This is hellebore," he said to Jonas, showing him a sachet. "It's the antidote to madness. I picked it myself at the summit of the Himalaya. Here is the manna that nourished our ancestors in the desert for forty years; it has all imaginable tastes. It was a priest's in Jerusalem whom I had saved from the plague who made me a gift of it in gratitude. Since the emergence from Egypt it had been transmitted in a sealed bottle from father to son, and from male to male, in order of primogeniture. This is my elixir of long life, which I compose myself with the marrow of an antelope, the bile of a giraffe and the brain of a sphinx. This is the Racahout des Arabes. This is the Eau de Rob,[1] which makes hair grow on the soles of the feet. This . . ."

"Oh, Sire Jerosonimo," cried the merchant, "you are a unique man, a sublime genius; you alone can save my little Rebecca; deign to look at the poor child, who is suffering incalculable ills!"

Doctor Jerosonimo remembered the object of his visit then; he turned to the bed on which Rebecca lay and advanced toward her at a slow, grave, majestic pace.

"Nature," he said, "engenders ills without number, but science dominates nature and breaks its decrees. Give me your hand, my child."

Rebecca obeyed.

The doctor placed his thumb over the large vein, counted the pulsations, blinked his little dark eyes and seemed to reflect. Then, looking at the child, he said: "Your tongue."

She opened her mouth and showed her beautiful teeth, as white as pearls.

Jerosonimo bent over, secured his spectacles, and darted a glance into the depths of the throat. Then he shook his head, and in a hollow voice, he said: "It's serious."

In the meantime, Esther and Jonas made a thousand grimaces. When he said "It's serious," the merchant raised his hands to the sky in mute despair.

---

1 "Racahout des Arabes" and "Eau de Rob" were patent medicines that enjoyed a brief fashionability in the early nineteenth century. The former, derived from acorns, supposedly bore some resemblance to chocolate and is still used as a cooking ingredient; the formula of the second was secret, known only to the pharmacist in Rouen who invented and marketed it.

"It's serious," Jerosonimo repeated, "but there's still a remedy . . . one, only one. You're fortunate, Sire Jonas, to have addressed yourself to me. No one else would have been able to fathom the mystery of this malady."

"Oh," cried the old man, "save my child, and my gratitude will surpass all the bounds of my poor fortune."

The doctor scanned the splendid furniture of the room with his gaze, and smiled. Then he said: "My beautiful child, what are you feeling?"

At that question, Rebecca dissolved in tears. "I'm feeling . . . I'm feeling . . . ," she said, in her soft voice, "dizziness . . . desires to yawn . . . my heart is suffocating, and when I eat, I feel sick."

Jerosonimo's face took on a singular character of suspicion. He fixed a hawk-like gaze upon the young woman, and an ironic smile creased his lips.

"I'd like to be alone with Mademoiselle," he said to Jonas.

As the father hesitated, he showed him a wisp of gray hair, the last vegetation of his bald and sterile pate.

Jonas and old Esther went out, but they remained behind the door. Then the wily doctor leaned toward Rebecca and said to her in a confidential manner: "Since when has the young man been coming?"

"What young man, Sire?"

"The one who loves you."

"Christian?" she said, with an astonished expression. "You know Christian? He didn't come yesterday."

"That's sufficient," said the doctor.

He went to the door and opened it. "You can enter, Jonas, I have good news to tell you. Your daughter is out of danger."

"Ah, God be praised!" cried the merchant.

"Yes, rejoice. The Lord said to our forefather Abraham: *your posterity will be as innumerable as the stars of the sky . . . as the grains of sand of the sea shore.*" At the same time he whispered a few words in his ear.

The merchant leapt into the air as if a whiplash had been applied to his buttocks. He raised his fist against the doctor and cried: "You're lying! My daughter is incapable of . . ."

"She has just confessed it to me herself," said Jerosonimo, coldly.

"She's just confessed it! That's impossible!"

Jonas leapt toward the girl's bed, saying to her: "Isn't it so, my child, that he's lying?"

"What?" she said. "What has Sire Jerosonimo said?"

"He says . . . he says . . . that . . . you've confessed . . ."

"I haven't confessed anything, Father."

"Eh! I was sure of it," cried Jonas. "She hasn't confessed anything."

"What?" said the doctor. "Haven't you agreed that a young man, a certain Christian, was the author . . ."

"The author of what?"

"Of your accident."

"My God," said the child, with a charming naivety, "Christian is the cause of my yawning? Oh, that's true— I'm very sad when he doesn't come."

"When he doesn't come!" howled Jonas. "He comes, then? He has come?"

"Yes, quite often. In the evening we chat, and we laugh together."

"Oh, wretch! Wretch!" cried Jonas, tearing his robe. "And you, old scoundrel, why didn't you warn me what was happening?"

In his fury he seized Esther by her gray hair.

"Eh?" cried the old sibyl, in a piercing voice. "Haven't you always said to me that Rembrandt's son was a superb fellow?"

"Rembrandt's son!" cried Jonas. "Rembrandt's son! I recognize the finger of God!"

At the same time he ran to the door and started traversing the city like a madman.

The doctor, Esther and Rebecca thought that the poor man had lost his head.

Jonas headed for the Rue des Juifs.

Everyone stopped to watch him run; his legs, as long as stilts, stretched out behind him; his large nose was directed forwards; his pointed hat was inclined over his neck; his dressing-gown was inflated by air. One might have thought him a stork launching itself from a roof and making efforts to rise up; there was nothing, including his floating sleeves, lifted up by long bony arms, that did not give him the appearance of that singular bird.

Jonas came to collapse in Rembrandt's courtyard.

VIII

Rembrandt had said to his son: if you don't tell me where my paintings are, you'll die of starvation.

That terrible threat was about to be accomplished. For forty-eight hours Christian had not received any nourishment; lying on the floor, pale and haggard, as livid as a specter, the poor fellow was no longer kicking the door; he could no longer stand up.

Rembrandt, sitting in the corridor, as weak and dejected as Christian, but of an inflexible will, his gaze burning with a somber fire, repeated from time to time: "Speak, wretch, where are my paintings? You'll receive a morsel of bread."

Only the echo of the vestibule responded to his hollow voice. Then he got up, applied his ear to the door, looked through the keyhole and murmured very quietly: "He's not responding. Perhaps he's dead!"

Involuntarily, his hand sought the key in order to open the door . . . then he sat down again, saying: "I'm fasting too! It's him who's obstinate. Oh, hunger . . . hunger! What suffering it causes!"

Rembrandt threw himself back against the wall, closing his eyes and biting his lips.

"Wretch! If he wanted to talk, we could eat! The thief has my paintings . . . he has them . . . yes . . . and he doesn't want to return them. The brigand! To borrow five hundred ducats! Five hundred ducats! Well, let him perish. I wish it were over already."

However, other thoughts occurred to the miser then. His own suffering gave him an idea of the young man's.

What he loved the most, after his gold, was Christian; that paternal affection was so great that he had not been able to inflict the ordeal of hunger on his son without suffering it himself. In his moments of tenderness he cried: "Christian! Christian! Confess, and I'll forgive you! We'll eat roast meat together, we'll drink porter . . . I'll forget everything, Christian."

Toward midday pangs of hunger took possession of him. He stood up, saying: "I can't stand it any longer."

It was then that the door opened and the exasperated Jonas appeared on the threshold.

At the sight of that man, to whom he attributed his son's fault, Rembrandt's face took on a terrible expression. If he had not felt weak, unable to walk, he would have hurled himself at the old Jew's throat, in order to strangle him.

For his part, Jonas was no less furious. His long, thin face, furrowed by wrinkles, expressed indignation and despair. His daughter's accident had put him in a rage, which his run through the city, by exposing him to the jeers of the crowd, had further augmented.

To see the two men, one tall and thin, with an elongated neck and an enormous nose, the other short and thickset, his jaundiced eyes flashing, one might have thought them a heron at grips with a hawk.

"Master Rembrandt," cried Jonas, "your son is a wretch; he has dishonored my daughter, my little Rebecca, an angel of purity and innocence."

"And you," said Rembrandt, "you, old rogue, you've dragged my son into disorder, you've lent him money. May Satan strangle you, along with your Rebecca, you old thief!"

"I'm not demanding my money," said the merchant, "Although I've advanced your son a thousand ducats."

"A thousand ducats!" howled Rembrandt. "That's false—you've only lent him five hundred."

"In justice," replied Jonas, "I can produce my titles. But it's not a matter of that."

The miser had become livid. "A thousand ducats," he said—and in spite of his weakness, he tried to hurl himself upon the Jew, but his strength betrayed him; he fell back on the chair, repeating: "A thousand ducats!"

"I won't insist on that sum," said Jonas, "if your son consents to embrace the religion of Moses and to marry Rebecca."

"What?" said Rembrandt. "What, my son become a Jew . . . are you mad, you old rogue?"

"Your son has seduced my daughter. He's the father of a child who . . ."

Rembrandt uttered such a cry of rage that even the second-hand dealer trembled at it.

"Get out, get out of here, usurer, get out, or I'll tear you to pieces."

Exasperation gave him an incredible strength; he launched himself at the merchant in order to strangle him. Defending himself, the latter recoiled all the way to the door. They were both howling, shouting dementedly, pronouncing fragmentary words and struggling in such a fashion that the house was shaken by it.

However, the old Jew, attacked head on, succeeded in the course of the brawl in opening the door. Standing on the first step he extended his long arms into the vestibule, and in a solemn voice he proclaimed: "Master Rembrandt, my poor old man, whose son has dishonored his white hair, I, the unfortunate, am only asking something just of you, which you reject brutally, without having regard to my age and my tears; I curse you! Yes, I curse you unto the twentieth generation. May you be poor, jeered at and despised! May Iblis establish himself in your dwelling and devour you!"

At the same time, he traversed the courtyard, covering his bald head with a flap of his robe, because he had lost his pointed bonnet in the battle.

Exhausted by that effort, his mind troubled, Rembrandt ran to Christian's room and opened the door. The latter had risen to his feet at the noise of the fight. His father took him by the hand without saying a word. He took him to a cupboard, cut a loaf of bread in half, and gave it to him. Then he dragged him to the door and shoved him outside, saying:

"Never let me see you again. You no longer have a father. I no longer have a son."

IX

At first, Christian did not understand the full extent of his misfortune. After taking a few steps along the walls, he sat down on a boundary-marker and ate the bread that Rembrandt has given him. Then he went to a drinking-fountain at the corner of the Rue des Juifs and drank avidly. Strength returned to him then; his pale cheeks were colored with an animated hue, his breast dilated and all his confused ideas were classified.

The disappearance of Rembrandt's painting, his anger, the torture he had inflicted on him, the apparition of Jonas, the words exchanged between the Jew and his father, and the struggle that had followed were all retraced in a striking manner in Christian's mind, like the memory of a dream initially forgotten. He also recalled the painter's words: "Never let me see you again. You no longer have a father. I no longer have a son."

Where could he go now? What remained for him to do?

The canal passed close by. Christian cast his eyes upon it; he even approached it and seemed to reflect; but the water was black and muddy. He turned away saying: "If it were Schiedam, or porter . . . there would be pleasure in drowning, but like that it would be necessary to have lost one's head."

Christian headed mechanically toward the Tavern of the Free Mercenaries. He found a numerous society there: Van Eick, Van Hopp and several others. They all received him with loud cries of joy, inviting him to drink, to eat, to gamble. Someone presented him with a glass. He sat down and told them naively what had just happened.

Then a singular change took place in the attitude of those joyful comrades. Gradually, they drew away from him; his glass was empty and no one had the idea of filling it.

"Damn it," exclaimed Van Eick, insolently, "you're telling us ridiculous stories; you owe me a revenge for the day before yesterday, and you're giving me a bad defeat."

Christian swore, affirmed and stormed in vain; everyone turned against him.

"In any case," cried Van Hopp, "supposing that Sire Christian is telling the truth, I find it very indelicate on his part to dare to present himself here without money, and to accept glasses of porter that he can't return."

"That's true," said the others. "His conduct is ignoble."

At the same time, Van Eick made a gesture, and Dame Catherine came to take away the young man's glass.

The fires of shame and rage rose to Christians face; his jaws clenched convulsively; the torture that was inflicted on him was a thousand times worse than that of hunger. He stood up and launched a terrible gaze at the wretches.

"You're cowards," he said to them. "You're insulting me because I have no more money."

"That's right," said the stout Van Hopp, with his stupid laugh. "You have a rare penetration, my lad. But if you follow my advice, you'll hurry up and leave, or we'll comb you like a donkey to teach you to live."

Christian went out cursing heaven and earth. He was already far away when their bursts of laughter were still pursuing him.

This time the poor fellow had the serious idea of running to the canal, but another thought occurred to him.

He walked aimlessly, his head bowed and his ears dangling, murmuring: "Yes, yes! Jonas has gold. The law of Moses is severe, but it's necessary to go that way. The Devil of an operation! If little Rebecca weren't so pretty . . . in any case, one little piece of flesh more or less doesn't change a man. It's not like the tip of the nose. My father doesn't want to see me again. If I go back, if he grants me mercy, it'll be the life of a damned soul: no more porter, no more Schiedam, no more cards, no more dice-cups. I'd a hundred times rather swallow the canal. By the soul of Satan, it's fate that will decide; I'll abandon myself to it. I'll throw myself at Jonas' feet and declare to him that the light of Mount Sinai has penetrated my soul."

In the meantime, night had fallen, and, as if by chance, Christian found himself in front of Jonas' house. He went around it several times, climbed over the garden wall and repeated the usual signal—but this time, there was no response; old Esther had doubtless been dismissed.

For more than three hours Christian walked in the avenues, raising his eyes to the façade, looking at the stars and the moon, outlining the lacework of foliage with its pale rays. The cold became intense. Christian was desperate. Finally, he seemed to see a light snaking along the windows. It was only a suspicion, because the closed blinds did not allow any ray of light to emerge from inside. In spite of that he approached the door and put his hand on it. It yielded.

Immediately, the fortunate Christian told himself that the door could only be open in order to let him in. Joyfully, he started climbing the stairs in darkness, and headed for his mistress's room. But as he set foot on the landing, a door opened at the end of the long corridor and Jonas, in a nightshirt, with a lamp in his hand, headed in his direction.

The young man's first impulse was to flee, but he did not have time, for the old man was walking with a surprising rapidity. Christian flattened himself against the door; he hoped that Jonas would pass by without perceiving him; but, having arrived opposite him the Jew stopped and stared at him, his mouth taut, his eyes wide open, but dull and glaucous, devoid of intelligence: the eyes of a cadaver.[1]

At that sight, Rembrandt's son was gripped by an unspeakable horror; his hair stood on end, and his teeth chattered. He tried to utter a cry, but his voice expired in his throat.

After a momentary pause, Jonas, without pronouncing a word, without a single fiber or muscle of his long face quivering, continued his nocturnal ambulation.

Christian had understood that there was a mystery in that; the thought immediately came to him to discover what the Jew was doing. He followed him step by step, endowed with a courage beyond his habitual character— or, rather, dominated by fatality. He marched behind the merchant as if drawn by the same current.

Jonas was trembling; his long, naked, jaundiced legs making immense strides. He opened the large oak door and launched himself into a dark room.

When Christian entered that room, he thought he was seeing the interior of a cathedral, so vast, spacious and high-ceilinged was it. Jonas' lamp could not illuminate its extent; it shone like a dot in the immensity. At the same time, a strong odor of paint rose to the young man's brain, and on the oak paneling he perceived a large

---

1 In 1849 Karl Ludwig von Reichenbach had not yet published his book on the "odic" force, to which he attributed the phenomenon of sleepwalking, but he had undoubtedly begun to develop it, and the mysterious aspects of the phenomenon were a current topic of debate, linked by some speculators with demonic possession. Jonas' somnambulism, however, cannot explain how he gets in and out of the houses he pillages, unless it is a mere side-effect of supernatural aid.

number of paintings, disposed symmetrically. They extended from the vault to the parquet.

Jonas launched himself toward a long ladder; he climbed it as a cat might have done, only making use of one hand and raising his lamp with the other, which projected and enormous shadow into the depths of the edifice. Having arrived at the summit of the ladder, the old man stood up, and illuminated with his lamp a corner of the vault, where Rembrandt's painting, *The Sacrifice of Abraham*, was visible.

On seeing the second-hand dealer in that perilous position, his back arched and thrown backwards, Christian could not repress a cry of terror:

"Jonas! Jonas! What are you doing? Be careful!"

At that voice, which resounded in the edifice, the merchant turned round . . . and then he vacillated, and tried to cling on to the wall, but his fingernails could find no purchase; he lost his balance, and dropped his lamp.

Plunged into darkness, Christian heard an impact, followed by a muted groan.

Rembrandt's son felt a chill in the marrow of his bones, and a cold sweat ran over his limbs; his legs buckled beneath him. He succeeded in regaining the door, but then he fell to the floor and remained unconscious for a long time.

Several days passed. Jonas' windows no longer opened; a deathly silence reigned in the vast dwelling. The municipal authority of Leyden, informed of the fact, ordered that the

Jew's house be searched. Then the second-hand dealer's cadaver was discovered in the midst of his magnificent gallery of paintings. It was already decomposing.

Astonishingly, a large number of the remarkable works composing Jonas' collection were recognized by the artists or collectors to whom they had belonged. All of them declared that the paintings had been taken in different epochs in an astonishing, inexplicable manner. The alderman made their restitution.

Rembrandt recovered his *Philosopher in Meditation* and *The Sacrifice of Abraham*. He recalled that the merchant had sold him his house, and suspected some secret passage communicating with the exterior, but all his searches in that regard were fruitless. At least the death of Jonas reassured him for the future.

Christian and Rebecca had retired to Bruges; they were living there in good intelligence. Rembrandt's son became a miser like his father; the welcome of his good friends Van Eick and Van Hopp at the Tavern of the Free Mercenaries had taught him the value of money.

A PARTIAL LIST OF SNUGGLY BOOKS